Caught Up in A D-Boy's Illest Love 3

TN Jones

Acknowledgment

First, thanks must go out to the Higher Being for providing me with a sound body and mind; in addition to having the natural talent of writing and blessing me with the ability to tap into such an amazing part of life. Second, thanks most definitely go out to my Princess. Third, to my supporters and new readers for giving me a chance. Where in the world would I be without y'all?

Truth be told, I wouldn't have made it this far without anyone. I truly thank everyone for rocking with me. MUAH! Y'all make this writing journey enjoyable! I would like to thank everyone from the bottom of my heart for always rocking with the novelist kid from Alabama, no matter what I drop. Y'all have once again trusted me to provide y'all with quality entertainment.

Enjoy, my loves!

TN Jones: Readers, thank you for tuning into the final installment of Caught up in a D-Boy's Illest Love. I have Casey, Jonsey, Jonzella, and Totta in the studio with me today. Thank y'all for taking time to sit with me today.

Casey, Jonsey, Totta, & Jonzella: You are welcome.

Jonsey & Jonzella: Thank you for having us.

TN Jones: Honestly, I don't know where to begin. There is so much I want to ask, yet, I don't because I don't want to give anything away. I guess I should ask ... Jonsey and Jonzella, what is really going on with y'all's father?

Jonsey: All I can say is the bastard has lost his damn mind.

Jonzella: (shrugs shoulders as she looks at her sister) I have to agree with my sister. I am at a loss of words behind what he has done, and what he is capable of doing.

TN Jones: Do you think y'all are safe from him?

Totta: (chuckling) All I have is three words for that motherfuckin' nigga ... The Savage Clique.

TN Jones: (Looks at Totta curiously) Are you referencing to X and her crew, Totta? If so, what do they have to do with Jonsey and Jonzella's father?

Jonzella: TN, that answer will be later in the book.

TN Jones: Oohhkay. So, now to the relationship questions. I will start with Casey and Jonsey, first. Are y'all going to make things work?

Casey and Jonsey: (both shrug shoulders without looking at each other)

TN Jones: Welp, no need in me pressing the issue there. Totta and Jonzella, how are things going between the two of you?

Totta and Jonzella: Good. Excited about the baby, of course.

TN Jones: Oh, yes, congratulations to y'all by the way. Casey and Jonse--. (I was cut off by Totta and Jonzella shaking their heads rapidly while mouthing no). Umm, well, it seems that everyone is tight lipped about what is going to happen. S--

Totta and Jonzella: Flip the damn page and begin reading with your nosey asses. (laughing after they finished their statement)

Chapter 1
Totta

Wednesday, February 15
Evening

As I strolled out of the police department with my lawyer beside me, I was highly confident that those funky ass detectives weren't able to put a case against me. It was too much heresy from "unknown persons" that speculated that I had something to do with Erica's condition.

"You enjoy the rest of your day," my lawyer stated as I waltzed towards my mother's vehicle.

She was standing behind it smoking a cigarette.

"You do the same," I voiced as we shook hands.

Parting ways, I wondered what my mother was going to say. I knew without a doubt I wasn't going to admit that I did try to kill Erica. There were some things my mother absolutely didn't need to know.

"What was said?" she inquired when I was inches away from her strong, beautiful frame.

"A bunch of speculation," I lightly voiced, glaring into her face.

"Come on and let's go. We'll talk about it on the way home."

"Okay," I replied before she moved towards the driver's door while I made my way towards the passenger side.

On the ride to my mother's crib, I told her what took place once I made it to the precinct. Even she said they didn't have a case against me. After her statement, silence was strong amongst us.

Not used to her being silent for so long, I asked, "Ma, what are you thinking about?"

"You getting your life together. These streets don't mean you no good. Settle down with Jonzella and be a happy family man. If you can't do that, then don't drag her into this mess, Joshua. Do you understand what I'm saying to you?"

"Yes, ma'am."

"Does Jonzella know what is going on?"

"No," I replied at the same time my cell phone rang.

My mother didn't respond as I pulled my cell phone out of my front pocket. Seeing Jonzella's name on the screen, my heart raced.

Answering the phone, her sweet voice greeted me.

"Hey. Where are you?"

"Heading back to my mama's crib."

"Okay. Tell her I said hello."

After I relayed Jonzella's message, Mama said, "IIi, sweetheart."

I didn't have to ask Jonzella did she hear what my mother said since I was sitting not far from her.

Clearing my throat, I said into the phone, "I'll be there in a few. I gotta chop it up with my mom's for a minute."

"Okay," Jonzella lightly voiced before we ended the call.

As I placed my phone in my lap, Mama said, "She's a good girl, Joshua. Do the right thing when it concerns her feelings."

"Yes, ma'am."

I knew that Jonzella was a good girl. There was no way in hell I was going to hurt her. Even though I tried to sabotage what we had; I was thankful that I was able to repair the slight damage that I caused.

As my mother turned into her driveway, she said, "We don't have anything to talk about, so take yourself to your pregnant woman and let her know what is going on."

Nodding my head, I kissed my mother on the jaw and exited her vehicle. Jumping into my whip, I started my engine, followed by me calling Dank. My call went unanswered so I dropped my phone in my lap.

Reversing from my mother's yard, I blew the horn. As I placed my gearshift in drive, I saw her waving. Zooming down the street, my mind traveled to Jonzella. It was short-lived as my phone rang.

Hoping that it was Dank, I quickly looked at the screen on my phone. Slight disappoint hit me once I saw Danzo's name.

Snatching up the phone, I answered it.

"Yo'," I spat in the phone.

"What in the hell you don' got yourself into now?"

Playing dumb, I asked, "What are you talking about?"

"Don't play with me, nigga. Why the detectives strolled up to your mom's crib on some humbug shit about that bitch Erica?"

I knew it wasn't going to be long before word hit the streets about the bullcrap I was involved in.

"What you heard?" I inquired with a blank face as I turned off the main street from my mother's neighborhood.

"That you tried to kill ole' girl, stuffed her body in the woods, and some other shit."

"That's the same thing that the detectives said I did," I voiced, chuckling.

"Why in the hell are you chuckling on a matter like that?" he asked, curiously.

"Because I find the shit funny. I'm trying to figure out where in the hell I had time to do that. Given, I hadn't seen the bitch in while. Mane, a bunch of he say she say shit going on. I ain't falling for that. Ain't no telling who out to get Erica, but it sure as hell ain't me. Knowing in that crazy broad, she probably paid someone to do some to her and try to have the shit blamed on me."

"Mmm hmm. I don't know why you was fucking around with the broad anyways."

"Just somethin' to do."

Snickering, Danzo said, "You need to find a better something to do. Put your dick and fingers in a pussy that is beneficial, ya', feel me?"

"Hell yeah. I'm done with these broads, mane. My lil' shawty pregnant and shit. I'm gonna settle down with her. "

"What!" he yelped.

As if he could see, I nodded my head while saying, "Hell yeah. Ah nigga got a little one on the way. I really believe that's why Erica trying to come after me. She learned that my lil' shawty is pregnant and shit."

As Danzo spoke, I zoned out to focus on a dark gray SUV with tinted windows. Seven lil' young niggas from my mom's hood were posted in front of it.

Quickly scanning the well-known yard which was cluttered with people and trash, I paid attention to the young gangsters' body language. Instantly, I knew that they weren't on any bullshit, yet they were toting pistols and heavy artillery.

Lil' C flagged me down causing me to tell Danzo to be quiet and listen to the conversation I was about to have with someone.

Pulling over, I made sure to have my tool in my lap. Rolling down the window, Lil' C strolled to the passenger window.

"What up, Totta?" the tall, caramel nigga stated as he leaned in the window and dapped me up.

"Shit, coolin'. What up?"

"Shit...a nigga just had to tell you that some niggas from the Nawf side inquiring about you and shit."

"Who were they? How many? What was said? What the body language was talkin' 'bout?"

"Erica Lickson's folks. Three of them. Them niggas body language got them fucked all the way up. We had to put that pressure on them niggas, feel me?"

"Good, good. Lock this side of town down. Stay alert and hit me up if shit get too sticky. Good looking out, my nigga," I informed him as we dapped each other up.

"A'ight. Be safe, my nigga."

"Always," I replied before he stepped away from my whip.

"We got some shit we need to take care of, huh?" Danzo voiced, clearly bringing me to realization that he was on the phone.

"Yep. Keep your eyes and ears open. I'll call you back."

"Bet," he replied before we ended the call.

Going above the speed limit, I made it to Jonzella's neighborhood within three minutes. Not wanting to park my car at the ladies crib, I decided to leave it at Dank's grandmother's crib. I was glad that no one was outside; I wasn't in the mood to chat with anyone other than Jonzella.

Jogging to her crib, I was ecstatic to see her sitting on the porch. She did something to me, and I loved the way I was feeling.

"You okay?" she voiced as she stood with her arms outstretched.

"I'm not sure," I told her as she wrapped her arms around me.

"We need to talk," I voiced seriously as I looked into her brown eyes.

"What's wrong?"

"Some shit popped off with Erica, and folks saying I got some to do with it which got some of her peoples at me," I told her as she pulled away from me, sighing heavily.

Shaking her head, Jonzella glared at me with a raised eyebrow.

"What?"

Not responding, Jonzella walked off on me, mumbling.

As I waltzed behind her, I said, "I don't need no fucking attitude from you, Jonzella. If you think I'm still fucking with that broad, you are out of your damn mind. It's just me and you...I mean that shit!"

"Every time I turn around that bitch and you are into some shit. What is it now, Totta?" she yelled, turning around to face me.

"I'm a suspect in an attempted murder on her," I replied as I strolled towards her.

Gasping loudly, Jonzella strolled towards me with her eyes bucked.

As soon as she approached me, she leaned to my left ear and whispered, "Well, did you have something to do with it?"

Without a moment's hesitation, I wrapped my hands around her waist and whispered into her ear, "Yes."

CHAPTER 2
Jonzella

A part of me was shocked that Totta actually told me the truth about him having something to do with the attempted murder of Erica. I was expecting for him to deny it. Since he didn't, I respected him for that. I knew that he was on the path of letting me further into his life.

Before I said another word, I led him into my room. I didn't want to say a piping word in the hallway; given, I didn't know what type of shit Jonsey was on.

The moment I closed my bedroom door, I began twiddling my thumbs as I asked, "What are you going to do about this situation?"

"I already have my lawyer on it. There's no way I'm going to be taken away from you and our child over some he say, she say shit," he voiced before clearing his throat, followed by placing me in his warm arms.

Silence overcame us as I thought about the whore who was trying to destroy my relationship. Immediately, I was pissed at him for not sealing the deal on the bitch's life.

Ring. Ring. Ring.

As Totta reached into his front left pocket for his phone, I tried my best to see who was calling. My task was unsuccessful as he pressed the answer button, followed by placing the phone to his ear.

"What's up?" he spoke while rubbing my back.

With the phone being on his left ear, I couldn't hear who was on the other line.

"I'm at the ladies crib," my man replied.

Without a doubt, I knew who he was talking to.

Sighing heavily, I hoped Casey didn't come over. I surely didn't want to hear him and Jonsey arguing.

"A'ight," Totta replied before the call ended.

"Dank on his way over here," Totta replied, glancing at me.

"Okay," I voiced as I bit down on my bottom lip.

Bringing his face closer to mine, I rubbed the left side of it before licking his lips. In a split second, I parted them with my tongue. While sharing a passionate kiss, I slid my body on top of Totta's chocolate frame. Gently palming my ass, Totta groaned in my mouth at the same time I felt his dick tap my pussy.

"Can I have some?" I asked after I broke our kiss.

Chuckling, he inquired, "Now what kind of question is that?"

Shrugging my shoulders, I smartly replied, "A question."

Flipping me onto my back, Totta didn't respond verbally to my statement. His actions spoke loud and clear. As he pulled my black shorts and pink, laced panties off, my man glared at me. I wasted no time removing my white T-shirt as Totta slipped two fingers inside of my hot twat. My body became rigid as he snaked his fingers through my moist pleasure box.

"Shittt," I cooed as I relaxed against the warm pillow, all the while throwing my pussy against his skillful fingers.

In a matter of seconds, my back was arched as I purred his name.

"Damnnn, you're super wet," he groaned before taking my right nipple into his mouth.

My eyes rolled while my body began to shake.

"Give me that nut, Jonzella," Totta whispered before licking in between my breasts.

Wasting no time, I gave him what he asked for.

"Ahhh," I moaned as I pulled on the pillows.

"Good girl," he chuckled, sliding further down my torso.

Is he finna taste my box? I asked myself excitedly.

My heart began to race as I was anticipating him tasting me. It was something he didn't partake in often. The further my man's face traveled south, the more I wanted to smile. Totta blew on my pussy, and I damned near leaped off the bed.

Laughing as he spread my legs wider, he questioned, "Mane, what's wrong with you?"

"Nothing," I lied with a smile on my face.

With his eyes locked on mine, I watched him stick his tongue out, followed by him licking on my aching pink bud.

"Ooou, Tottaaa!" I whimpered.

With his fingers still inside of me, Totta took his time tasting me. Careful sucks, tugs, licks, and finger fucks drove me crazy.

Placing my hands on the back of his head, I fucked the hell out of his fingers and tongue. Removing his fingers from my pussy, I wanted to taste my juices; thus, me, bringing his fingers to my mouth. Totta had a mouthful of pussy as I sucked on his fingers. When he groaned, the vibrations from his mouth rippled through my pussy, causing me to moan along with him. On the verge of cumming, I squirmed while holding onto the back of his head.

"My Godddd!" I cooed with his fingers in my mouth.

Totta continued his mouth services until I begged him to enter me. I was itching to feel his dick banging inside of me. I needed that dick something awful!

"You love rushing shit, chill, Jonzella. I'mma give you what you want," he voiced sternly as he lifted his mouth from my pleasure box.

Fifteen minutes later, Totta had me making all types of noise, along with running from his mouth and fingers. Out of my four sexual partners, none of them made my body sing the way Totta had mine singing melodies and shit.

After he removed his mouth from my pussy, I was eager to suck on his tongue. Pulling him to me, I slapped my lips against his. As we engaged in a sloppy kiss, Totta began unbuckling his belt. He wasn't successful for the simple fact that I was dry humping the shit out of him. I couldn't control the hunger that I had for us to make love. He had to pop my thighs for me to stop humping. Finally, he was naked. Tapping his dick against my pussy, I huffed and puffed. I was beyond impatient, and he knew it.

"Calm down, you finna get this dick," he chuckled while looking at me in a naughty manner.

"Then stop playing with me, and give me what I want," I whimpered against his lips, all the while gazing into his dark brown eyes.

Gently sliding his dick up and down my moist pussy, I moaned. Biting his bottom lip, I made him put the dick in me. Soon as it entered my hot hole, I was cumming.

"Got damn," he groaned as he slow rocked my body.

Not in the mood for fucking slow, I said, "Fuck me, Totta."

Doing as I commanded, Totta took my body on a ride that I had been waiting for. Every corner he touched had me creaming on his penis and praying that his loving didn't stop.

While we were tearing up my bed, the doorbell chimed.

Knowing who was at the door had me thrusting my cat on my man, so that he knew he had to get his nut as well as providing me with mine. While we serviced each other with pure bliss, I prayed that Jonsey and Casey wouldn't fuck up my nut.

"That's Dank. We gotta make this a quickie, baby," Totta told me as he lifted my legs over my head.

Instantly, I felt uncomfortable which made me frown. He was getting ready to open his mouth when Jonsey knocked on the door and said, "Totta, Casey's in the front room for you."

"Okay. Tell him I'll be out in a minute."

"K," she replied before relaying the message to Casey.

Lord, please don't let her act a fool, I thought as Totta noticed the look on my face.

Slowing his pumps, Totta asked, "That hurt?"

"No, it was just uncomfortable."

"You want me to hit this pussy like that?" he questioned as he slow rocked the right side of my twat, causing my muscles to clench.

"Hmm, hmm," I whined.

Dropping his body closer to mine, Totta had me singing like a canary and dripping wet. In no time, we came together. As his penis pulsated, Totta's body relaxed against mine.

"You know I love you, right?" he asked while glaring into my eyes.

Nodding my head, I said, "I think so."

With a frown, he spat, "What the hell you mean you think so?"

Shrugging my shoulders, I didn't say anything.

"You think I'mma eat your pussy and not love you?" he questioned.

Once again, I shrugged my shoulders.

"I'm not a pussy eater...I'm a dick slanga. So, in order for me to be eating your pussy damn near for thirty minutes...I must love you," he stated before removing himself off me.

"Hmph," I replied sarcastically as I looked at him.

Being a dick slanger was the reason he was looking at an attempted murder charge.

"What's up with the sarcastic response?" he inquired as he put his boxers and jeans on.

"Nothing," I voiced with an attitude.

Throwing his shirt over his head, he replied, "Don't start no shit, Jonzella."

"I ain't," I stated as I hopped out of my bed, going towards my dresser.

Trying my best not to get mad at him, I savagely grabbed undergarments. Standing behind me, Totta planted kisses on my neck as he reached in the drawer and pulled out a pair of dark gray boxers.

Heading out of my room, we greeted Casey. Totta informed him that he was going to take a shower, and then they could talk.

As I slipped in the bathroom, I wondered why Jonsey wasn't talking to Casey. I knew I had to see what she was thinking.

Our shower was a short one. Afterwards, Totta went to the front room, and I slipped into Jonsey's room.

Plopping down on her bed, I asked, "Why aren't you talking to Casey?"

"I could tell that he didn't want to be bothered so I'm not going to bother him," she replied as she was flipping through the TV channels.

"Regardless if he looks like he doesn't want to be bothered, you should tell him about the pregnancy."

"I'm not going to keep it," she stated seriously as she looked at me.

With bucked eyes, I sighed heavily. I didn't know what to say, so I remained quiet.

As she placed her head on my shoulder, I felt warm tears. Knowing that she was hurting, I held my sister as she began to cry.

"Everything will be okay," I told her, not sure if I was telling the truth.

Chapter 3
Casey

When I arrived, I was expecting for Jonsey to tell me that she was pregnant. To my surprise, she didn't. As she disappeared to her room, I couldn't take my eyes off her. She was beautiful as ever with puffy, red, wet eyes. I wanted to ask her what was wrong, but I kept my questions and comments to a minimum—hey, was all that I said when she opened the door.

Seeing Totta trying to hand me the blunt brought me into reality. As I grabbed it, he began telling me about his day with the detectives. Hearing him say that he was a suspect in trying to kill one of his flunkies, I choked on the weed smoke.

"Damn, woe, it's been a while since you got choked like that," he laughed.

It took a while for me to stop coughing. When I did, I had questions for him.

"What is the lawyer saying? What the detectives had to say? Why in the hell didn't you make sure the bitch was deceased? How are you going to handle this heat man? You about to be a daddy, woe."

"It's he say, she say. There is no evidence against me. My lawyer said I have nothing to worry about. I need to either shut the naysayers up or prove that the bitch wants to see me in prison since I don't want to be with her."

"Basically, you need to flip things around and make her look like a vindictive bitch?" I asked as I passed him the blunt.

"Exactly," he voiced before tugging on his favorite smoke.

Silence overcame us as we looked around the quiet, lightly lit, one-way street. No one was outside that I could see, just the way I liked it. I wasn't too big on having people staring me in my face as I chilled outside.

"You should go and talk to her," Totta voiced as he handed me the blunt, referring to Jonsey.

"I told you, I'm good in that department," I stated sternly as I shook my head at the blunt he was holding.

"Are you really?"

"Nope, but I'll be okay."

Shaking his head, my partner left the conversation alone. Jonzella's voice was the reason why we didn't say a thing. Eavesdropping was one of our best qualities.

"I'm hungry," she growled.

"That ain't shit new," Jonsey stated as Totta nodded his head.

"Let me see what this woman wants to eat," he voiced while standing.

"A'ight."

Opening the door, he looked back at me and said, "Are you coming in or not?"

With a puzzled look on my face, I was debating whether I should go in. Totta asked me again, and I hopped to my feet. Knowing that I should stir clear of Jonsey, I couldn't. I didn't have to talk to her, but I had to look at her. Crazy, I know, but I didn't want her out of my eyesight, for the time being that was.

While they talked, my phone was vibrating in my pocket. Retrieving it, I saw Trasheeda's name.

Quickly answering the phone, I had my eyes on Jonsey as she was sitting at the kitchen table thumbing through what looked like *The Bulletin Board* book.

"What you doing?" Trasheeda asked me as Totta asked Jonsey a question.

"Chilling. What's up?" I quickly replied to Trasheeda's question.

Jonsey and Totta were talking. About what? I had no damn idea since I was on the phone with Trasheeda.

"You coming over tonight?" she inquired happily.

"Yeah."

"Around what time?" Trasheeda probed.

"Not sure yet. I'll call you when I'm on the way."

"Okay," she stated before we ended the call.

I ended the call at the right time to hear what was on Jonsey's mind.

"Jonzella, I think it's time for us to move into separate homes," Jonsey stated in a blank tone.

"Wow," Jonzella voiced in a shocked timbre before continuing, "Now, where in the hell did that come from?"

"You and Totta deserve y'all own space, especially since y'all are going to be parents," she voiced while circling some things in the advertisement book she was looking in.

The room became quiet as I held my eyes on Jonsey. It took Totta to speak for the eerie silence to be broken.

"Y'all wanna watch a movie or something?" he inquired.

"I'm cool with that," I stated as Jonzella agreed.

"You cool with it, Jonsey?" Totta asked, glancing her way.

"I'm getting ready to head out. Maybe I'll catch another one with y'all."

"Where are you going?" Jonzella asked curiously.

"Need to clear my head," she voiced as she stood.

Continuing, the beautiful lady said, "Check out the things I have circled. You might like them."

Sighing heavily as she nodded her head, Jonzella replied, "Okay."

As Jonsey strolled towards her room, she made sure to keep her eyes off me. I thought she was going to say something smart since I had my eyes on her, but she didn't.

Totta, Jonzella, and I made small talk as they fixed them something to eat. Shortly afterwards, Totta put a movie into the DVD player. I didn't care to know what he put it since I wasn't going to be there long. I wanted to know where in the hell Jonsey was going; I prayed that she would tell her sister where she was headed.

Forty-five minutes later, Jonsey was fresh out of the shower and dressed to impress. I wanted to ask her where in the fuck she was going, but I didn't open my mouth. Waltzing past me, Jonsey's sweet-smelling perfume filled my nostrils. Instantly, my dick was bricked.

"You dressed the fuck up...where are you going, Jonsey?" Jonzella inquired with a raised eyebrow.

With her left hand on the door as her right hand was pulling down her car keys, she said, "Don't wait up."

As soon as the door closed behind her, Jonzella shook her head, followed by grabbing her phone. It didn't take her long to become frustrated. Throwing her phone down, she was angry as hell.

I wasn't into the movie at all, and with Jonsey gone there was no need in me being present.

After Totta and I dapped, followed by me saying goodnight to them, I exited the duplex. On the way to my car, I pondered where Jonsey would be going on a Wednesday evening.

Taking a seat in my whip, I started the engine on my whip and pulled up Jonsey's Facebook account. Seeing that she hadn't posted in a few days, I sighed heavily before closing out the app and reversing from her residence.

In need of getting deep throated and slamming into some pussy, I zoomed to Trasheeda's home. Along the way, I prayed that Jonsey wasn't on the verge of doing anything stupid that would cause me to go off on her ass. I would hate to put my hands around her pretty, thin neck!

Fifteen minutes later, I was pulling into Trasheeda's nicely decorated yard. As soon as I cut off the headlights, her front door opened, and she was standing in the door looking extremely fuckable as she wore the hell out of a red, tight-fitted dress.

Placing my phone on vibrate, I exited my car. As soon as I placed my right foot on the concrete, my stomach began to rumble from the wonderful food aroma escaping out of Trasheeda's home.

"What you don' cooked, woman?" I inquired as I closed my car door.

"Steaks, baked potatoes, and I made a Greek salad," she sweetly replied.

"Hmm, sounds delicious."

"Would you like something to eat?" she voiced as I leaned in for a hug.

"Yes I would," I replied as she planted a kiss on the left side of my neck.

Normally, I wouldn't eat at Trasheeda's, but tonight I wanted to switch things up a bit. Plus, I hadn't had anything to eat since this morning.

Thirty-five minutes or so of me being in her home went smoothly as we chatted about what we had going on. Once the polite conversation ended, Trasheeda got down to business with my dick in her mouth; I had to say that I was very impressed. She was giving a nigga some super sloppy toppy. My eyes were rolling in the back of my head, mouth wide open, hands balled up, and toes curled until I believed I popped all my toe knuckles.

"Shit, girl, you doing the damn thing," I groaned as I grabbed the back of her head.

In between slurping on my dick and moaning, Trasheeda was lightly kneading my balls. A nigga was in heaven with the warm, wet sensations her mouth was providing.

Zit. Zit. Zit. Zit.

In my pocket, my cell phone was vibrating. In an intense moment, I wasn't going to answer the damn thing. After several more vibrations, my device stopped only to start back vibrating again.

My body grew stiff as my nut rose to the tip of my dick. In a matter of seconds, I sounded off with, "Shit...swallow all that shit, girl."

Slamming my dick as far down Trasheeda's throat as I could, I burst down her throat.

With her eyes on me, she removed her mouth followed by saying, "Did you enjoy?"

"Woman, you know I did," I responded as she stood.

"Good. Now, relax and get that dick ready for round two," she commanded before strolling towards the hallway.

Zit. Zit. Zit. Zit. Zit. Zit

Pulling my cell phone from my pocket, I saw that my grandmother was calling me. Sliding my hand across the answer option, I answered one of my favorite lady's calls.

"Hello," my soothing deep tone spat in the phone.

"Someone just shot up my home. Where--," she stated before I cut her off as I quickly hopped to my feet, fixing my clothing.

"I'm on my way," I voiced angrily as I exited Trasheeda's home without saying a word to her.

She was on my heels asking me where I was going.

Ignoring Trasheeda as she came to the front door, my grandmother told me that her and my mother were okay.

"Grandma, y'all go to my house. I'm headed to your home now."

"Okay," she voiced before we ended the call.

The moment I hopped inside of my whip, I started the engine and peeled away. As I approached the first stop sign, I dialed Totta's number. On the fourth ring, he answered the phone.

"Yo'."

"Aye mane, somebody shot up my grandmother's crib. Meet me there."

"Are you fucking serious?" he asked in an angry timbre.

"Yep."

"Woe, I'm headed there now!"

"A'ight."

"One thing I know for certain, whoever just blasted at my fam's crib...ain't gon' live to shoot up nobodies else's shit," I voiced.

"You motherfuckin' right they ain't. I'm leaving as we speak," Totta voiced.

"A'ight."

Ending the call, I was mad as hell as I turned the volume up on Kevin Gates "Can't Make This Up".

The call ended. There wasn't much to say. All that would be discussed would be in person, especially after knowing someone was out to get him.

CHAPTER 4
Jonsey

I didn't have a destination in mind when I decided that I wanted to leave the house. All I knew was that I wanted to get away from Casey. I had to clear my mind and figure out what I wanted to do with my swollen uterus. I know I told Jonzella that I wasn't going to keep it; however, I felt that was wrong of me to even think about getting rid of an embryo that didn't ask to be made.

Ring. Ring. Ring.

Looking at the screen on my phone, I saw Jonzella's name. Rolling my eyes and sighing at the same time, I answered my sister's call.

"Hello," I stated as I watched customers' food being served.

"Hey, where are you?"

"IHOP."

"Are you alone?" she inquired curiously.

"Yes," I replied as a thin waitress stepped to my table.

Instantly, I told Jonzella to hold on while I placed my order. Within ten seconds, my order was placed and the waitress was on her merry way.

"Talk to me, please," Jonzella whined.

"There is nothing to talk about."

"Are you really going to have an abortion?"

"I'm indecisive about it," I voiced as a gorgeous eye candy of a guy caught my attention as he strolled in with four guys—all handsome, might I add.

Shit, he fine as hell, I thought as Jonzella said, "What has you indecisive about the situation?"

"I don't want to talk about that right now."

"Okay."

The line went silent as my eyes kept staring at the average height, light-skinned, tatted, shoulder-length dread head dude. The moment he found me looking at him, I dropped my eyes to the table and told Jonzella that I would talk to her later.

Ending the call, I placed my cell phone on the table. At the same time, I felt eyes on me. Slowly lifting my eyes away from the table, I saw Mr. Eye Candy glaring at me. His medium beaded peepers held my attention as I felt myself squirming on the warm seat. As I cleared my throat, he stood. I tried to break the eye contact but he had me hypnotized. I couldn't look away!

Taking a seat across from me, he extended out his hand and said, "Hi, I'm Jotson, and you are?"

My God, that gold in his mouth setting him off, I thought as I felt my body tingle.

"Jon...Jonsey," I voiced shyly as I placed my hand into his.

"It's nice to meet you, Jonsey."

"Likewise," I replied nervously.

"I just wanted to stop by and get your name since you kept staring at me," he snickered, showing a mouth full of gold teeth.

Blushing as my eyes were low, I replied, "Sorry. You are very good looking. I didn't mean to glare at you the way I did. I bet you are used to women doing that, huh?"

"Yep," he stated with a slight smile on his face.

Silence overcame the table as my waitress brought my food.

"Thank you," I replied before she asked Jotson would he like a menu.

"Yes, please," he responded.

Nodding her head, she said, "Sure thing."

The moment the waitress left, Jotson began inquiring about me. Every single question he asked, I answered honestly—well, minus the question of whether I had a guy in my life.

The waitress returned with his menu. Jotson didn't take it from her hand before saying, "I will have what she's having down to the orange juice."

"Okay. I'll go place your order in, sir," she voiced happily before skipping away.

"What do you want to know about me?" he voiced, giving me his full attention as his homies called his name.

After seeing what they wanted, his attention was back to me. With a raised eyebrow, Jotson repeated his question.

Stammering, I finally responded with, "Whatever you want me to know."

Within ten minutes, I knew the basics about him. Where he went to school, how many siblings he had, what his hobbies were, how old he was, and no children or girlfriend but he had a couple of female friends. For some strange reason, I felt jealous about him admitting that he had a couple of female friends. I knew well what that meant.

After we finished eating, he asked, "Where are you going once you leave here?"

"I'm going to cruise the streets."

"Ah, someone doesn't feel like being in the house."

"Not really."

"Well, I don't feel like going home either. Maybe we can cruise the streets together until you are ready to go home," he announced while glaring into my eyes.

"That's cool, but um I'm driving, and you are riding with me."

Laughing, he said, "Shid, that's cool with me, Ma."

Jotson placed a twenty dollar bill on the table before saying that he's paying for my meal as well. I told him that I would take care of my ticket, but he wasn't hearing that. After he gave me a stern look, I didn't say another word about paying for my food. Before we left the restaurant, he chatted with his homies.

On the way out of IHOP, Jotson asked, "Do you feel comfortable trailing me to my crib so that I can drop my whip off?"

Without hesitating, I said, "Sure."

I knew I had just met him or whatever, but I felt comfortable around Jotson. It was his cool, laid-back vibe that drew me to him. I didn't feel like I was in danger or that he was a stranger. It felt as if I've known him for quite some time. As I followed him to an unknown destination, I was excited about hanging out with him. He was the perfect remedy for me not thinking about Casey or being pregnant.

Five minutes later, we were pulling into Sunshine Village Apartments.

"Oh, so he doesn't live far from me," I voiced aloud as my cell phone began to ring as we pulled into a low-key apartment complex off Atlanta Highway.

Seeing my mother's name displaying across the screen, I didn't waste my time answering the phone. As it continued to ring, I shoved it inside of the armrest.

Jotson slowly drove to the back of the apartment complex, followed by making a sharp right turn into a vacant parking lot.

Coming to a complete stop behind his vehicle, I didn't unlock my doors until he was reaching for my door handle.

As he hopped in the front seat, I had a slight smile on my face.

"Let's enjoy the night, shall we?" he asked as I pulled away from his resident.

"Yes, we shall," I voiced as K Camp's song "Own Boss" played at a nice decibel.

We cruised through the streets of Montgomery for over two hours, chatting and laughing. The entire time we hung out, our cell phones were ringing off the hook. Neither of us paid our devices any attention. Growing tired of driving, I asked Jotson to take the wheel.

Doing so, he asked, "We have been all over this city and the country area. Where are we going next?"

"I don't know."

Silence.

"How about we chill at my crib?"

Nibbling on my bottom lip, I thought heavily on the answer. I didn't want to go home, yet, I didn't want to give him any indication that we were going to have sex. That surely wasn't going to happen.

He must've sensed what I was thinking because his statement was, "I won't do anything to you. I'm just enjoying your company.

It's obvious you don't want to go home, and I don't want to be alone. So, what do you say, Ms. Jonsey?"

In a low voice, I replied, "Sure."

Thirty minutes later, Jotson was parking my car beside his. Grabbing my cell phone out of the armrest, I exited my vehicle as Jotson locked it. Scrolling beside him, I was a nervous mess. My mind was screaming for me to go home, yet, I couldn't go. I didn't want to face my issues. I didn't want to cry myself to sleep.

Soon as he unlocked and opened his front door, Jotson said, "Welcome to my crib."

Jotson gave me a tour of his one-bedroom apartment. He had it decked out nicely. I was impressed with his furniture selection and choice of colors.

I was surprised to see that he had a lot of pots and pans. I didn't think single men cooked like women did. Yes, he showed me where the utensils and cookware were located, which I found that to be weird. Yet, I didn't ask why he showed me where they were located.

After the tour was over, we decided that watching TV would be great. As he flipped through channels, we quickly learned that OnDemand was our best option. It took us a while to find something that we really wanted to see. There weren't any movies that caught our attention; thus, we decided to catch the latest season of *Shameless*.

Ring. Ring. Ring.

Our phones sounded off, and we didn't even look at them.

Kicking off my shoes, I tucked my feet underneath my butt. The temperature seemed to have dropped drastically; thus, me shivering.

"Are you cold?" Jotson asked as he looked at me and licked his lips.

Nodding my head, I thought, *My God. Those damn lips just did something to me.*

"Would you like a cover?"

"Yes, please," I voiced while fumbling with my fingers.

Hopping to his feet, Jotson waltzed upstairs. In no time, he was back with a black, cotton bedding cover. After kicking off his all red Jordans and pulling off his red Jordan shirt, Jotson placed the cover over me, followed by taking a seat and throwing some over his body.

"May I hold you?" he quickly asked.

"Yes," I replied before scooting close to him.

Placing my head in the crook of his arm, I felt Jotson's athletic body relax.

"Are you comfortable?" his soothing voice asked in a low timbre as he gently rubbed the left side of my body.

"Yes," I stated as I nodded my head while placing my eyes on his.

"Good," he replied as he brought his head closer to mine.

Knowing that I should've pulled away, I didn't. Our lips connected, followed by our tongues clashing together. The kiss we provided each other was sweet and tender. His long, thick pink flesh explored my mouth as I moaned—completely enjoying the sensual kiss. It took him to break the kiss because my ass would've let it lingered.

"That is as far as we are going to go...let's watch this show, Ms. Jonsey," Jotson groaned as I felt his erection.

Oh, my damn! He got a tool on him, I thought as I said, "Yes, please, let's do that."

CHAPTER 5
Totta

Thursday, February 16ᵗʰ

Ever since Dank arrived at his grandmother's crib, we had been on the hunt for the person or persons that shot up his grandmother's spot. It took us forty-five minutes to get the answers were sought after. After learning the individuals names, we knew them very well. They were the same niggas that Lil' C said was looking for me; they were baby dope boys from the North side.

With the proper identification of the niggas that shootup my homie's grandmother's crib, we had to find their residence. Now, that was an issue since the guys didn't have a crib of their own. They bounced from house to house; yep, those jokers were homeless want to be dope boys.

After an hour of finding the place they rested their heads, Dank and I put together a plan that would aid us in keeping the fuck niggas and anybody else riding for Erica quiet. While we waited on the fuck boys to appear, we caught a eyeful of shit that I wished we hadn't.

"I know damn well that wasn't Jonsey that waltzed up in Jotson's crib," Dank voiced as he dropped his cell phone in his lap and sat upright in the driver's seat of his cousin, Tremaine's whip.

"Yep."

"Aye man, call Jonzella and tell her to call her sister to see where she at," he spat with an attitude.

"A'ight."

Doing as my homie commanded, I wasn't in the mood to be dealing with no female shit. I was on the hunt for the niggas who shot up his grandmother's crib.

"Hello," Jonzella spoke.

"Aye, baby. Can you do something for me?"

"Yes."

"Call Jonsey and see where she at?"

The line went quiet before she said, "Why?"

"Dank wants to know."

"Oh okay," she replied before telling me to hold on.

In a matter of seconds, I heard a ringing line. Placing the phone on speaker, I looked at Dank. The look he gave told me everything that I needed to know. He was on some stupid shit!

As soon as Jonsey's voicemail sounded off, that nigga was damn near blue black in the face.

Jonzella ended the call, and I thanked her. Before I ended the call, I made sure that she knew I was going to come back once I handled my business.

"I want to know why in the fuck she in the house with that nigga...at this time of the motherfucking morning," my homie spat as he pulled out his cell phone, proceeding to dial her number.

"Dude, we ain't got time to worry about that. We are on a stakeout, my nigga. Deal with that shit later," I hissed while shaking my head.

As he growled, I knew that nigga was pissed off to the max. Pulling his tool from underneath the driver's seat, I had to slam that nigga's back into the driver's seat.

"Aye, nigga. You ain't finna roll up in ole boy shit because yo' lil' pussy in another nigga's crib. You the one that said you was gonna leave her alone. So, what you mad for?"

"My nigga, she pregnant with my seed and she at another nigga's crib. The fuck you think!" he yelled angrily while looking at me.

"Oh, now you truly acknowledging the fact that she's pregnant. Yet, you was in her face and didn't make her talk to you. Mane, you on some mo' shit right now. Get your head in the game."

Dank was on the verge of opening his mouth, until the car we were seeking pulled right beside us. Out hopped the niggas that were seeking me. Those silly jokers were standing around the car talking and smoking.

"Mane, I can't wait to find that nigga Totta. I'mma peel his motherfuckin' dome all the way back. He fucked with the wrong female. Ain't no nigga gonna do my family like that," the driver, Dev, stated quickly.

"Aye, y'all leave them guns and shit in the car. I don't want Nana saying nothing about them in her crib. You know she be up late and shit...checking my room and shit," Pooch stated.

"These some goofy ass niggas," Dank whispered as he reached underneath his seat.

Not responding to his statement, I followed suit as he placed the silencer on his gun. We patiently waited for the fuck boys to exit from the parking lot. We had a nice setup waiting for them soon as they met the front door.

Ten minutes later, the dummies began walking towards the door.

"You ready?" I asked Dank as I placed the ski-mask over my face.

"Shid, you already know this," he replied as he quickly dropped the black ski-mask over his face.

I knew Danzo and Tron were ready to get off the ground; they had been down there for over two hours. They were underneath bushes by the front door. Danzo was on the right side as Tron was on the left side.

As Totta and I slowly opened the car doors, we aimed our weapons at the fuck niggas. In a flash, shit jumped off. Those niggas didn't see us coming as their bodies dropped to the ground. Not a sound was made by them, just the way we planned it.

Soon as the job was done, Tron and Danzo ran to Danzo's truck. As Dank started the engine on his cousin's vehicle, I fired up a cigarette while hopping into the passenger seat. Pulling away, we never looked back or said a word.

"Dank, where in the fuck are you going?" I questioned quickly as he didn't follow Danzo, which was a part of the plan.

"Shit, I forgot we supposed to be following them niggas," he replied, turning around in the middle of the road.

Shaking my head, I chose to keep quiet. I didn't want to set his ass off, which would result in us arguing in the car. The moment we get settled, I was going to let that nigga have it. The ride to Waugh, Alabama, was silent. That was normal for us to be quiet after a kill. We had to make sure that we did everything the right way and left nothing behind.

Once Danzo and Tron hopped in the car with us, we resumed to our normal selves.

"Mane, did you see how them niggas' bodies dropped like flies being sprayed with Cutter spray?" Danzo asked before laughing, which caused me to laugh at the rehashing of that sight.

Dank was extremely quiet as we laughed about the murder that was committed. I knew that my homie was feeling some type of way; thus, I asked him was he okay.

"Yeah, I'm good. Aye, hit yo' ole lady up and see if Jonsey reached out to her."

Nodding my head in response to him, I called my lady.

"Hello," she yawned.

"Hey, baby. I'm on my way to you."

"K," she stated.

"Dank wants to know have you heard from your sister?"

"No. I guess she turned her cell phone off. It's going to voicemail. I'm starting to worry about her."

"Nawl, don't worry about Jonsey, she's fine," I stated, not really wanting to say that in front of Dank.

"How do you know?" Jonzella inquired curiously.

Clearing my throat, I looked at Dank before saying, "I saw her with someone."

"Who?" Jonzella questioned.

Before I got a chance to answer, Dank yelled, "She gon' get fucked up. I ain't even playing around with her ass no mo'."

"What in the hell is he talking about?" Jonzella asked as Tron and Danzo started cracking on Dank for his reaction.

"She with a dude named Jotson."

"Oh, well...damn," Jonzella replied.

"Yep," I stated as Dank went off the moment I said that nigga Jotson's name.

"Aye, baby, I gotta go and calm this nigga down. I'll be there soon," I voiced loudly, trying to out talk my pissed off homeboy.

"Okay. Be safe."

"Always," I responded before ending the call.

"On gawd, I'mma drop down on that nigga soon as I see his ass!" Dank angrily voiced as I sighed heavily while shaking my head.

***

I was awakened by Dank going off on Jonsey.

"Lawd, let me get up and make sure this nigga don't do shit stupid," I sighed as Jonzella rolled towards me, followed by glaring into my face with her crusty eyed ass. Even with the crust in her big brown eyes, my baby was still beautiful.

Sighing heavily, she replied, "I think I need to get up as well. Jonsey can be unpredictable at times."

As we lifted our bodies from the bed, Dank shouted, "So, you ain't got shit to say, Jonsey!"

The moment Jonzella opened the door, I saw that my homie was beyond pissed off as he pinned Jonsey down on the sofa. They were face-to-face, yet I saw that Jonsey had a nonchalant facial expression.

"So, you just gon' fuck another nigga while being pregnant with my seed, huh? You think that shit cool or sum?"

"First of all, Casey, who in the hell said anything about me fucking another dude? Secondly, who said anything about me being pregnant?" Jonsey replied coolly.

"Mane, look, I know what type of nigga Jotson is. I'm a street nigga just like him. We do the same types of shit. Fuck bitches and go on about our business as if we don't even know them!"

This nigga don' said some shit that he ain't got no business saying. What in the hell is he thinking? I thought as Jonzella and I stopped at the threshold of the hallway which led to the front room.

Jonsey began chuckling for quite some time, which I didn't see anything amusing. Dank didn't say anything while she laughed; he just stared at her while shaking his head.

Jonsey stopped laughing, followed by saying, "Hmm, so, you fuck bitches and go on about your business and act like you don't know them afterwards, huh? We fucked several times. You and I aren't talking or fucking at all. So, tell me why it bothers you *if* I did fuck Jotson."

Seeing Dank's jaw muscles clenching, I knew he was choosing his words wisely.

"Mane, look, what are we going to do about the baby situation?" Dank voiced lightly as he removed himself off Jonsey and sat beside her.

"I've been heavily thinking about having an abortion. I'm not completely sold on it, but I think it is best. I want to finish school, find a career, and *not* be tied down to a nothing ass nigga like yourself," she spat casually while staring my homie in the eyes.

The wind was knocked out of my chest the moment I saw his head drop low. One thing Jonsey didn't know was that Dank loved the hell out of her. It was her outburst that caused the split between them, even though she tried to apologize and make things right between them.

Pulling out his cell phone, Dank scrolled through his device.

In a matter of seconds, we heard a soft voice say, "Reproductive Health Services. I'm Meagan. How may I assist you?"

Jonzella and I looked at each other. Her eyes were bucked as I shook my head.

"Hello, Meagan. I would like to know the process of a woman having an abortion," Dank voiced as he placed his back to the sofa while placing his mobile device in his lap.

The woman told him what must take place before the procedure was done. He asked about the costs and she told him.

Once the call ended, he looked at Jonsey and said, "Whatever you decide to do, call me so that I can do my part, give you the money."

"Okay," she replied blankly as her cell phone rang.

The moment her phone was in her hands, Jonsey's entire attitude change. She had a huge smile on her face.

Swiping her index finger across her screen, Jonsey happily said, "Hey."

Dank turned to face me, followed by cocking his head to the right. Jonsey was happily chatting her ass off. Without a doubt, I knew who was responsible for her sudden attitude change. If I knew, I knew Jonzella and Dank did as well.

"Um, I was disturbed out of my sleep but yeah I can be ready in forty-fi--," she stated before Dank snatched her phone from her hands and smashed it against the wall.

"You got me fucked all the way up, Jonsey! You think I'm just gon' let you and that nigga be? Shid, you must don't know I love killing motherfuckers when they fuck with what's mine!" he yelped as he shoved her against the crook of the sofa.

"Let's go, Dank!" I voiced sternly as I quickly strolled towards the sofa.

"I ain't finna hurt her, mane. Her and I got some shit to discuss," he voiced while glaring in her facc.

"Nawl, we don't have shit to discuss. Why don't you go and discuss some shit with the bitch that you had at your house...yeah, the same bitch that you dissed me for when I tried to make things right with between us!" Jonsey spat coolly.

"Look, don't play with me, guh!"

In a blink of an eye, shit went left the moment Jonsey punched Dank in the face. She two pieced his ass.

His balled fist was in the air as I yanked his ass from the sofa. If I was ten seconds late, he would've knocked Jonsey's ass out!

"Yeah, it's time for us to go!" I voiced sternly as I had a battle with getting him out of the house.

All I wanted to do was play inside of my girl's pregnant pussy, not be dealing with this nigga and his unstable ass feelings, I thought as we argued and wrestled to his car.

CHAPTER 6
Jonzella

Once the guys left, Jonsey hopped to her feet.

"Where are you going? We need to talk," I told her as I was on her heels.

"I'm going to get me a new phone and spend the day with Jotson."

"Do you think it is wise to do so?"

As we entered her room, she nodded her head, followed by saying, "Shit, I don't see anything wrong with it. I'm single. He single. What's wrong with two *single* people mingling?"

"Jonsey, but you are pregnant."

"And after today, I will no longer be keeping this child. My mind is made up. I prefer to have a child with someone I'm going to spend the rest of my life with."

Before I could open my mouth, my cell phone rang. Quickly disappearing out of Jonsey's room, I dashed into mine. Retrieving my phone off my nightstand, I saw Renee's name on the screen.

"I don't have time for her shit either," I mumbled as I ignored the call.

As I made my way to Jonsey's room, Renee called me again. I ignored the call. Plopping down on Jonsey's perfectly made bed, I analyzed my sister as she decided on what she was going to wear. The silence was killing me, so I tried my best to spark up a conversation that wasn't going to make her shut down on me.

"Did you sleep with him?"

"Nope," she replied as she continued shuffling through her clothes.

"Are you lying to me?"

"Nope."

"Does he know you are pregnant?"

"Nope."

"Are you going to tell him?"

"Nope because I won't be for long."

In need of changing the subject to get a better reaction out of her, I brought up Renee calling me.

"You should talk to her. I keep telling you that."

"What in the hell are we going t--," I began to say before my phone rang.

Placing my eyes on the screen, I saw Dad on the screen. Immediately, my heart began to beat faster.

"Dad's calling," I said aloud.

"Then answer the phone," Jonsey stated blankly.

Shaking my head at her tone, I did what she said.

"Hello."

"Hi, sweetie. How are you and your sister?"

"We are good."

"That's good. I miss y'all. Y'all's mother said hello."

"Tell her we said hey," I replied, making it a point to not say that I missed him.

Sighing sharply, he announced in a low timbre, "Why are you talking to me like that, Jonzella?"

"No reason, Dad. I'm just tired," I lied.

Chuckling, he voiced, "That maybe a factor as well; however, I know better. I don't want anything to change between you, Jonsey, your mother, and me. Do I make myself clear?"

The way he spoke sent chills through my body.

As I nodded my head, I said, "Yes, sir."

"Good. When I call either of your phones...make sure that you respond within a timely manner as you girls have always done."

"Yes, sir," I replied in a shaky tone.

"Good. Now, y'all have a great day."

"You as well," I responded before the call ended.

Throwing my phone on Jonsey's bed, I said, "Dad expects for us to act like we don't know anything. From his tone, if we don't comply there will be some issues."

"Fuck him and his wife!" Jonsey spat as she held a pair of black jeans and a gold collared shirt.

Ring. Ring. Ring.

Glancing at my phone, I sighed followed by yelling, "Shit, she getting on my nerves!"

"Then answer the damn phone and get the shit over with," Jonsey's smart ass stated before skipping out of her room.

Answering the phone with an attitude, I rolled my eyes as Renee tried to make polite conversation with me. For the next twenty minutes, we argued. She wanted to spend time, and I didn't. She wanted to know why, and I refused to explain for the one-hundredth time why I didn't want to be bothered with her.

The back and forth shit was working my nerves; thus, I said, "Look, Renee, I forgive you, okay? I just don't want to talk to you nor see you. Just leave me alone. That's what you are good at doing."

"You ungrateful bitch, you! I should've swallowed your ass instead of having that nigga nut in me!" she yelled, catching me off guard.

Tears welling in my eyes, I growled through clenched teeth, "When I see you...it's on sight, bitch!"

"I'm glad you said that because I'm sitting on your front porch, lil' pregnant bitch!"

Dropping my phone, I ran to the front door. As soon as I opened the door, Renee was standing on the porch with a 'I dare you to fuck with me' facial expression. Little did she knew, I was about that life. I gave her ass the business on the porch. I boxed her ass out as if I was Mike Tyson. She had to learn that I was nothing to play with.

Mother or not, Renee was not going to disrespect me, period! Shoving my left hand around her neck, I began to apply pressure to the unwashed area. Swinging her arms wildly as I held firm to her neck, Renee made a choking sound.

Not giving two fucks, I slammed my right fist into her face repeatedly as I stated, "You gon' respect me, bitch! My mental is not wrapped too tight."

Tired of beating and choking her, I realized that she needed another type of ass whooping. Dropping my hands from her neck and face, I grabbed a fist full of her freshly done weave and began dragging her hollering ass inside of my home.

"Ahh! Let me go, Jonzella!" she yelled at the same Jonsey asked a question.

"What in the hell is going on, Jonzella?" she inquired as she ran in the front room, fully dressed.

"Jonsey, help me, please!" Renee yelled at the same Totta strolled into the house.

He was yelling as well.

"Jonzella, chill the fuck out!" my man demanded sternly as he pulled me away from Renee.

Successfully pulling me away from the bitch, I had three black tracks of weave in my hand.

Throwing them on her face, I yelled, "Get your raggedy, hoe ass up outta my shit. The next time you come here...I will shoot your ass in the face for trespassing!"

After Jonsey helped the bitch out of our home, Totta laid into me.

"What in the fuck were you thinking, mane? You actin' like you ain't pregnant. The next time you get into some shit with my seed in your womb...I'mma fuck you up."

Taking a seat on the sofa, I sighed heavily as Totta dropped to his knees in front of me. As he rubbed my back, I dropped my head in my hands and cried. I wasn't upset about beating on the woman that gave birth to me; I was upset about letting her get to me. I could've possibly miscarried fucking around with a nothing as woman.

"Stop crying. I'm done fussing at you. She didn't hit you, did she?" Totta spoke while kissing me on the right side of my neck.

"I didn't give her time to put her hands anywhere near my body, and I'm not crying because you fussed at me. I'm crying because I let Renee get the best of me while I'm pregnant," I sobbed.

"Do you want me to have one of my girl cousins whoop on her ass some more?" he asked seriously.

Wiping my face, I placed my eyes on my chocolate guy and laughed.

"You laughing, but I'm dead serious. I will not have anyone doing anything to piss you off, pregnant or not. Understand me?"

As I nodded my head, Jonsey ran in the house, followed by slamming the door and locking it—all the while looking annoyed.

"What in the hell is wrong with you?" I asked her as Totta took a seat beside me.

"Don't y'all let him in here. I don't have anything to say," she replied as she snatched her car keys from the key holder.

It didn't make sense for me to ask who she was talking about; it was apparent she was talking about Casey.

This bitch finna escape out of her window to get to her car, I thought as three knocks sounded off at the door.

"Jonsey, I want to apologize for my actions. I'm sorry. Whatever you choose to do about the pregnancy, I stand behind you. However, I meant what I said about you and that nigga, Jotson. He ain't no good for you. Trust me, I know."

Turning my face to his, Totta said, "We are not going to get in their business. They will figure things out for themselves. Understand?"

"Yes, Zaddy," I cooed as I lay in his arms.

"Don't start no shit that you can't handle," he voiced as he rubbed his chin in my wild tresses.

"Now, you know I can handle anything you throw at me," I voiced as I glanced at him.

"Well, since you say it that way...come throw that pussy on a nigga's tongue."

With a smile on my face, I hopped to my feet and ran to my room. He laughed from the time he left the front room until he waltzed into my room. I was naked in a flash.

With a raised eyebrow as he laughed, that fool said, "Umm, yo' ass been fighting and sweating. I don't want no sweaty pussy in my mouth. Fuck you think this is?"

Bursting out in laughter, I said, "Shit, you said throw this pussy on your tongue and I forgot I been out there wearing that bitch face out."

Scooping me into his arms, Totta carried me into the bathroom. As we passed Jonsey's room, I glanced in and saw that she wasn't in there.

Shaking my head, I said, "Well, my sister has escaped out of her damn window like we are teens."

"Since we are the only ones here, and probably will be for quite some time...how about we get real x-rated?" Totta stated as he placed me on the cold toilet seat.

"I'm all yours, Joshua Nixon," I cooed while rubbing the sides of his face.

"You better be or your ass gonna be stanking like them niggas that shot up Dank's grandmother's crib," he stated with a straight face.

"Explain, now," I voiced lightly.

"Let's just say that Erica's people came looking for me. They saw my car at Dank's grandmother's crib and assumed I was in there. Hence, the reason they shot up the house. Let's just say won't nobody be looking or fucking with me anymore."

The mention of him killing someone turned me the fuck on. I didn't know what was wrong with me, but I was one horny individual knowing that my man was a certified killer; meanwhile, I was afraid of my dad. Instantly, I had to reevaluate my thinking when it came down to my father. He had never done anything wrong to me, and neither had Totta. If I was willing to be Totta's woman, and I knew what he was capable of and has done, there shouldn't be any reason why I isolated a man that raised me from the age of seven.

"Baby, before we get started, I need to call my dad and apologize," I told him as I bit down on my bottom lip.

With a raised eyebrow, Totta asked, "Why in the hell would you do that?"

"There's no difference between you and him...if you catch my drift."

"Shittin' me. There's a big difference. That nigga murdered his own sons. I wouldn't dare kill my kids unless--," his voice trailed off.

"Unless what?" I probed as he turned on the water knobs.

Clearing his throat while standing erect, Totta replied, "Unless one of them has hurt you in a way that no child should do to their parents, loving parents at that."

"I highly doubt my brothers did anything to our mother, other than making her worry. You know what, baby, I'm not going to stress over my issues with my dad. It's all about you, our baby, and me. The rest of this shit I'll figure out along the way," I stated as I gave a weak smile.

"Don't stress. In due time, the answers you are seeking will come. Then, you can decide on what to do with your father," he voiced as he began to undress me.

"Okay," I replied as he brought his head closer to mine, followed by licking my lips.

Engaging in a passionate kiss, I slowly caressed his body as butterflies were floating in my stomach.

Breaking our kiss, Totta said, "I'm going to marry you. So, when I ask you...yo' ass better say yes. Now, let's enjoy our shower together before I put that ass to sleep."

CHAPTER 7
Casey

Friday, February 24th

"Boy, you working my nerves with all that walking around and shit. I'm ready to go back to my home," my grandmother stated as I dipped into the kitchen for something to eat.

"Grandma, I really don't want y'all at the house until I feel it's safe for y'all to be there," I told her as I fixed myself another bowl of cereal.

"My home is fixed, and it's safe for your mother and me to live in," she responded in close range of the kitchen.

Taking a seat at the kitchen table, my grandmother watched every move I made. I knew she wanted to talk, but I didn't. I wasn't the type to openly discuss my feelings, and I sure as hell wasn't up for a lecture from Geraldine.

After I fixed a bowl of cereal, I took a seat at the table. Sitting erect in the chair, my grandmother glared at me. I didn't place my eyes on her. Therefore, she took it upon herself to make me look at her.

"You haven't been my smiling Casey in over two weeks or maybe longer than that. What's wrong with you? Girl trouble? Are you depressed about what happened at my home? Was someone after you or Totta?"

After swallowing the morsels in my mouth, I kept my eyes on my food as I said, "Nothing is wrong with me, Grandma."

"You can't even look me in the eyes. I want to know everything that I just asked you about. It will stay strictly between us. As you already know this," she voiced, lightly tapping on the table.

Turning my head towards her, I continued to avoid eye contact, all the while sighing heavily.

"You know I want eye contact as we converse. Let's get this conversation over with. I'm ready to go home. You and Totta have been there for the past week fixing it up and whatnot."

As I placed the spoon in the bowl, I cleared my throat while looking at her. I exhaled sharply several times in hopes she would start her speech without me having to tell her the truth.

With wide eyes, she nudged me, followed by saying, "I have a bingo game to get to, so you need to spill the beans, honey."

"I was interested in this female. The one you saw at Wal-Mart some time ago. We were kicking it and all. Things went to the left. She tried to make things right, but my knuckleheaded ass was looking out for me and Totta...in case, she got angry and said some things."

"Oh, the young lady that blew up at your home," my grandmother stated as she kept her eyes on me.

Nodding my head, I softly said, "Yes."

"Go on," my grandmother stated after it took me too long to continue.

"I cut things off. I didn't want to, yet, I did. I found out she's pregnant. Yes, I'm responsible. She didn't tell me, Totta did. I had mixed feelings about it. That was until Totta and I saw her going inside of another nigga's crib last week. Afterwards, we had an argument about her dealing with someone else while being pregnant with my seed. She mentioned that she was thinking about having an abortion, and my petty ass called the abortion clinic in the city. I told her that whatever she chose to do, I would be there to support. Truth be told, I was semi-lying when it came down to the abortion part, but I didn't let her know that. Jonsey pissed me off one too many times and I raised my hand at her. Grandma, I was so pissed with her nonchalant attitude about the dude and the pregnancy that I was actually going to put my hands on her."

"Did you apologize to her?"

"Yes."

"Did she accept your apology?"

"I don't know. I had to apologize through the door. So, I'm not sure if she heard me or not."

"You need to control your anger when it comes down to a woman that you love. We will do shit that will piss y'all off. You gotta learn how to walk away before things get out of hand. Has she called you?"

"No."

"Have you called her?"

"I've texted her, but she hasn't responded," I voiced softly.

"Give her some space. If y'all are meant to be, y'all will be. Now, answer the rest of my questions," she demanded as she quickly glanced at the clock on my kitchen wall.

Ring. Ring. Ring.

Saved by the bell, I thought as my mobile device rang and vibrated on my hip.

"Don't think you aren't going to answer my questions, Casey," my grandmother spat as I pulled my phone from the holster.

Ring. Ring. Ring.

Seeing Totta's name on the display screen, I quickly answered the phone.

"What's up?" I spoke as my grandmother eyed me down.

"Shit. Coolin'. Tron and I set up the cameras around Miss Geraldine's crib. If she wanna come back home tonight, they good to go. I got some foot soldiers that's gonna keep an eye out on the house."

"A'ight. She been itching to come back home anyway."

"Well, she can. Have you talked to Jonsey?"

"Nawl. I texted her but she hasn't responded. How has she been? What is she talking about?" I inquired as I hoped she mentioned me and was talking with some sense.

"I don't know how she's been. She hasn't been home in some days," he replied.

Instantly, I grew angry.

"What do you mean she hasn't been home in some days? Has Jonzella talked to her?"

"She been staying with ole boy, and yes, Jonzella has talked with her. Every day, Jonsey calls to let Jonzella know she is okay."

Clearing my throat, I asked my partner several questions that he couldn't answer. Finally, I asked the right one, and it made me feel very sour.

"From what one of his homies is saying Jotson is really digging Jonsey. He ain't tried to smash or nothing. He's taking his time with her."

Shoving the bowl of cereal across the kitchen table, I hopped to my feet. Anger soared through me because I knew Jotson was going to be an issue for me. I didn't want anyone with Jonsey but myself. If I couldn't have her, he sure as hell wasn't. I meant that shit!

"Aye, I'mma holler at cha later," I told him before ending the call in a nasty manner.

"Fuck!" I yelled as my grandmother jumped.

"Sit down and calm your nerves, Casey. Now, finish telling me what I want to know."

"Yes, the guys that shot up your home were the same niggas that were heating at Totta about a chick that he dumped. We found their location and murdered them. No, I am not depressed. I'm angry that I fell for a woman whose brothers I was going to murder because they were a key witness in a beating. Their testimony could've landed me and Totta in prison for life. I'm mad as hell at myself for trying to get over Jonsey by pushing her away and being disrespectful when I invited a broad to my crib. All Jonsey wanted to do was make things right with me, and my stupid ass gave her my ass to kiss! How in the hell can I get my woman back without killing that nigga she been laid up with?" I spat as I realized that tears were streaming down my face.

I had broken down in front of my grandmother and I could barely look her in the face. Eventually, she told me that she was going home and for me to call her once I felt like talking. I was done talking since I spazzed out from learning about Jotson and Jonsey spending so much time together.

How in the fuck am I going to get her back? Shit, will she even take me back after the way I acted towards her? I thought as I glared at the kitchen wall.

"I don't give a fuck what I gotta do to get her back...I'mma get my woman back!"

***

Ring. Ring. Ring.

Picking up my cell phone, I saw Totta's name on the screen. Without hesitation, I answered the phone.

"Yo'," I spat as I let back the recliner.

"What's the move for tonight?" he asked, smacking on food.

"I'on even know. It's a Friday night, and I need to get out of the house before I lose my mind," I voiced as I placed the phone on speaker so that I could text Jonsey.

"How about we just hop on the interstate and ride?"

"Nope. I wanna stay in the city."

"Dude, it's a Friday night, and the last thing you need to be is in the city. You are bound to get into some shit, which will cause me to get in some shit."

Not hearing what my partner had to say, I hung up the phone, followed by hopping out of the recliner—aiming for the bathroom. There wasn't a soul that could tell me what I wasn't going to do. I didn't want to leave the city in case Jonsey called and wanted to talk to me. The last thing I need was for her to think I was entertaining whores when I was trying to make things right with us.

Ding. Ding.

As I ascended the stairs to the master bathroom, I quickly opened the text from the one person I had been waiting to hear from. I came to a complete stop as I read her text.

Ms. Lady: *There are no hard feelings, Casey. You moved on, and I should do the same. You can keep your money. I'll pay for the abortion myself. Take care.*

I was a mess as I rehashed her text as I responded.

Me: *I haven't moved on, Jonsey. I want you and only you. I even want the baby. Please don't have an abortion. I need you and my seed in my life. Come to my house so we can talk. All I want to do is talk and make things right.*

I waited patiently for Jonsey to text me back. After ten minutes of standing in the hallway, looking dumb as hell, I realized that she wasn't going to respond.

Sulking as I strolled into my bedroom, I had to find a way to get Jonsey in my face.

An hour later, I was strolling down my stairs--looking good and smelling great. Soon as I opened the door, Jonsey's sexy ass was walking away.

"Aye, Jonsey, where are you going?" I hollered as I ran after her.

"I shouldn't have come. I'm sorry," she replied as I grabbed her waist, slightly turning her around so that she could face me.

Brushing the wild strands of hair away from her face, Jonsey shivered as she cooed loudly.

Bringing her closer to me, I gazed in her eyes as I said, "I'm so sorry that I stooped that low as to raising my hand at you or making you feel less than. I really want to be with you and start a family with you. I don't see you being with anyone but me."

She searched my eyes, all the while biting on the lower portion of her bottom lip. Sighing heavily, Jonsey shook her head.

"Why are you shaking your head?" I inquired as I began to walk us towards the front door.

"I don't know why I'm here. I don't know if we are going to wor--," she stated before I cut her off by shoving my tongue in her mouth.

At first, Jonsey was hesitant on kissing me. Six seconds of me slowly maneuvering my tongue inside of her warm, minty mouth, she began reciprocating the kiss. While I grabbed Jonsey by her thighs, she wrapped her legs around my waist. We kissed as if it was nobody's business. My dick was harder than the Russian language as I strolled towards my front door. The passion left our bodies the moment some unwanted bullshit popped off.

"So, I guess I am a jump off for you whenever your young bitches don't do what you ask them too, huh?" Trasheeda yelled from behind us.

As I turned around to look towards the road, Jonsey slid down my body.

Jonsey shook her head while saying, "Wow."

"Jonsey, don't you leave!" I demanded loudly before questioning Trasheeda.

"What in the fuck are you doing at my crib, Trasheeda?"

As Trasheeda strolled further in my yard without saying a word, Jonsey was walking towards her car. Not knowing what was on Trasheeda's mind, I had to make sure she didn't put a hand on Jonsey.

"I asked you a fucking question, Trasheeda. What in the fuck are you doing at my crib?" I voiced loudly as I was in close range of them.

"I stopped by when I saw you kissing on this hussy. So, I guess you won't be calling me anytime soon to fuck and suck you since the little young bitch is back in your life," she voiced angrily while pointing at Jonsey.

Before I could open my mouth, Jonsey voiced loudly, "Y'all hoes kills me trying to come for me when you clearly have no room. You are the motherfucking jump off, bitch. If you think you are going to roll up on me then bitch, you better think again. I am the wrong motherfucking young pregnant bitch to piss off!"

The arguing started between them. While they argued, I noticed some of my neighbors standing on their porches as others stood on their grass looking at the scene. I failed miserably getting Trasheeda to leave my home and get Jonsey into my home. One too many wrong things were said out of Trasheeda's mouth, resulting in Jonsey pulling out a chrome .22 pistol from the small purse she was carrying.

Immediately, Trasheeda threw up her hands, followed by saying in a shaky timbre, "I don't want no problems. Dank, lose my number."

I didn't have time to respond to Trasheeda's remark because I saw the anticipation of Jonsey wanting to shoot after the broad. As Jonsey watched Trasheeda get in her car, I had to get the gun out of her hands.

The tires on Trasheeda's vehicle could be heard from the moment she left my curb until she turned onto the main street.

Knowing that I was in some shit, I tried to explain myself before Jonsey began going off on me.

"Jonsey, give me that g--," I voiced before she sternly looked at me.

"You shut your hoe ass up!" she barked while rolling her beautiful eyes.

Clearing my throat, I refrained from telling her to watch her fucking tone when speaking to me. I would correct her ass the moment I would get between her legs.

With a raised eyebrow, Jonsey glared into my face before speaking.

"At this moment, I don't want you to explain shit to me. I care less about what in the hell just happened. I don't want to know how long y'all have been fucking around or when the last time you slept with her. That's none of my business. What I want from you is very simple...to suck my pussy until I cream down your throat, followed by you sucking on my asshole and toes. Then I want you to fuck me all over this motherfucking house of yours. When we are done, then I will leave your property. Can you do that for me baby daddy?"

CHAPTER 8
Jonsey

Zit. Zit. Zit. Zit. Zit. Zit.

"Who in the fuck keeps calling you back to back, Jonsey?" Casey questioned as he pounded in my pussy.

"Ahhh!" I cooed.

I didn't giving a damn about my ringing phone. All I cared about was getting dicked down.

Casey plunged further inside of me, causing me to ram my head against the headboard. Grimacing from the head pain, I placed my hands on his chest. Slapping my hands away from his chest, Casey aggressively slid me down the bed, all the while glaring at me. The nasty look he gave me sent chills through my body, causing me to shiver. Within a blink of an eye, that black bastard delivered disrespectful, yet passionate long strokes to my dripping wet pussy.

That type of dick stroke caused females to stalk a man, flatten his tires, burst his windows out of his car and home, and to act as if she was stupid. That same damn stroke, also caused the best side effects, the shaking of the limbs as your eyes rolled in the back of your head, all the while screaming out the man's name.

"Cassseeyyy!" I screamed in pure pleasure.

Not wanting to take my eyes off him, I didn't. I wanted to see his facial expression as he punished me. Oh, the looks he gave me informed me that he was extremely upset with me. I didn't give a damn. He was the one that fucked up our situationship.

My mind stopped went blank the moment he lifted my left leg and slowly thrusted his dick in and out of me. My body craved more of him like it did the past six times we had sex since I arrived at his home.

"This pussy belongs to me. You belong to me. The baby I put in your womb belongs to us. I ain't going nowhere, and neither or you. Do I make myself clear?" he growled in my ear as he continued to slow stroke my pussy, hitting every corner that made me want to melt.

"Oooouuu," I whimpered as I dragged my nails across his back.

"Fuck that moaning shit, Jonsey. Did you hear what I said?" he questioned while pulling himself out of me, followed by slamming his dick back inside of me.

"Y...yesss," I groaned as my back arched.

Sliding his warm, sweaty palms underneath my back, Casey rode my pussy until I creamed on his penis.

As I flopped my body on the warm sheets of his bed, Casey spread my legs and slowly toyed with the opening of my super moist twat with the head of his dick.

"Jonsey, I'll kill that nigga Jotson if you in his face again. Do you understand me?" he questioned sternly while glaring into my eyes and massaging my breasts.

Whimpering as I breathed heavily, I nodded my head all the while thinking, *This nigga is truly crazy as hell. He thinks he's going to have his cake and eat it too...well, he got another thing coming fucking with me.*

Our sex session carried on for another thirty minutes. Once it was done, we showered together while he apologized for his behavior. While I poorly listened to him, I was thinking about Jotson. His smile, jokes, cooking, and how comfortable I was with him. I wanted to be in his arms; thus, I knew I had to escape Casey's home and run to the one that invaded my mind.

As I stepped out of the shower, Casey asked, "Are you hungry?"

"No," I lied as I felt a slight rumble of my tummy.

"What would you like to do tonight?" he asked as he turned off the shower, followed by stepping onto the big, white towel.

"I'm going home and getting in bed. I have to be to work at nine o'clock. So, no hanging out for me," I stated, semi-lying.

I did have to work but I sure as hell wasn't going home.

Sighing heavily, he replied with, "After all the fucking we just did, you have enough energy to drive home?"

"Yep."

"Look, I know you might be feeling some type of way about Trasheeda bu--," I stated before she cut me off.

"I told you I didn't want to hear anything about your business. I'm not feeling any kind of way about anyone. Since I'm still pregnant with your child I don't feel comfortable having sex with someone else right now. So, I came to you so that you could give me that nut that my pregnant body was craving."

The veins in Casey's forehead showed while he growled loudly. When he finally stopped growling, the words that left his mouth had me speechless.

"You gotta be the dumbest bitch on this Earth if you think I'm going to be your motherfucking jump off while you are happily entertaining that nigga Jotson. I'll tell you what, Jonsey, put on your clothes and get the fuck out of my crib."

While he stormed out of the bathroom, I was trying to find a way to close my damn mouth. Before I could dry off good enough, Casey threw my clothes, shoes, and phone at me.

"Hurry up and get the fuck out!" he yelled, which made me jump.

Tears began to well in my eyes as I scrambled to put on my clothes.

Zit. Zit. Zit. Zit. Zit. Zit.

Looking down at my phone, I saw that Jotson was calling me. Quickly ignoring the call, I continued putting on my clothes before I burst into tears in front of a man that I had no idea whether I wanted to be with him.

"Hurry up and get your ass out of here, Jonsey!" Casey barked as he put on the outfit he had on when I first arrived.

Growing angry with myself and him, I spat, "Keep being an asshole, and I promise you I will get the last motherfucking laugh!"

"Mane, get the fuck on."

Wiping the tears away that fell down my face, I exited his bedroom as my phone vibrated and rang. As I rapidly descended the stairs, I answered the call.

"Hello," I stated as casual as I could.

"Hey, you okay?" Jotson asked in a concerned tone.

"Yeah, I'm okay. What's up?"

"I wanna kick it with you tonight. Possibly we can go bowling or something."

"No, bowling. Pick another event," I voiced as Casey's heavy feet plopped down the stairs at the same time I opened his front door.

"How about we go out?"

"Nawl, I'm not feeling the club scene," I stated as I slammed the front door behind me.

Halfway to my car, that ignorant bastard stated loudly, "Make sure you tell that nigga you pregnant! I bet he won't stay interested in you long."

The line went quiet as I quickly unlocked the doors, followed by hopping inside of my chilly vehicle.

"Jonsey, you good?" Jotson voiced curiously as I started the engine.

"Yep."

"Was that guy talking to you or someone else?"

At that precise moment, I had two choices: come clean about being pregnant or not say a damn thing.

Sighing heavily, I said, "He was talking to me."

"Did you just find out or you been knew?"

"Been knew for some days now."

"That was your baby daddy?"

"Yep."

"I thought you weren't dealing with anyone."

"I'm not. Had to come and get my things," I lied as I reversed my car.

"A'ight."

An eerie silence overtook the phone as I left Casey's yard. It took a while before Jotson or I said anything. When he did speak tears flooded down my face.

"You cool as shit, and I like being around you, you know? Just because you are pregnant doesn't mean we can't continue to hang and enjoy each other's company. With that being said, are you on your way over here, woman?"

***

"So, what are going to eat, woman? What are you and the embryo craving for?" Jotson asked as he ran his left hand across his head as we played a racing game on his Xbox.

"Um, I think I'm in the mood for Mexican food," I voiced as I zoned into the game.

"As long as you don't stink up my bathroom like you did three nights ago," he joked.

Nudging him while laughing, I shook my head at his silliness. I couldn't lie as if that Mexican food didn't tear a sister's stomach up some days ago. I was in such a rush to get home that day that it was unbelievable. By the time I sat in the driver's seat, I was hopping out of my car clenching my ass muscles, praying that Jotson wouldn't judge me. Let's just say that I never shit at anyone's home but my own—well, until that night.

"It's okay, woman. Everybody shits," Jotson stated before bursting into laughter, interrupting me rehashing one of my embarrassing moments.

Shaking my head with a smile on my face, I said, "Let's continue this game, sir."

After several minutes of us trash talking, Jotson cleared his throat before saying, "Okay. So, I wanna know how you feel about the pregnancy?"

Thrown for a loop, I paused the game and stared at him. With a raised eyebrow, I bit down on my bottom lip as I didn't know how to answer his question. My stomach began to growl, which would cease the conversation—for the moment that was.

"Can we get our food first before we indulge in that conversation?" I asked while placing the game controller on the sofa.

Zit. Zit. Zit. Zit. Zit. Zit.

Ignoring my phone rang, Jotson said, "Nope. If I'm going to be in your life, I need to know how you feel about things. In case you haven't noticed, a brother digging you super hard. I love our chemistry, how you think, how independent you are, and that you are not like the other chicks that throws themselves at me. So, be honest with me Jonsey, please."

Standing while grabbing my small purse, I sighed heavily as I said, "I'm not sure how I feel about the pregnancy. One minute, I tell myself I'm going to have the baby, and the next I'm saying I'm going to have an abortion. I don't want to put my life on hold because I made a careless mistake or two."

As he put his controller down, Jotson grabbed my hand. We lifted off the sofa in silence. I didn't want to have this particular conversation with him. Hell, I couldn't have this conversation with myself. How in the hell was I supposed to tell him what I thought or wanted when I was indecisive?

While walking towards the front door, Jotson stated casually, "Just because you are pregnant doesn't mean I'm going to stop wanting to be around you If you decide to continue the pregnancy or abort the pregnancy, I will be here for you."

Nodding my head as he retrieved his keys from the dark brown, wooden key holder, a slight smile was on my face as I bit down on my bottom lip. The warmth that I felt in my heart was overwhelming.

God, thank you for sending him in my life. He is right on time, I thought as we stepped into the night's chilly air.

Unlocking his car door, Jotson said, "I meant everything I told you, Jonsey."

From the shadows, a woman said, "Yet, you fail to tell me that you were a certified player who didn't give a damn about anyone but himself, or that you play underneath vulnerable women like me so that you can get whatever you want out of them. Well, Jotson, you have fucked over the wrong female."

The way the woman talked scared the hell out of me. I didn't know what to expect from her; thus, I slowly moved away from the person, who at first I couldn't see. I didn't know who the female was, but I knew without a doubt that she was a scorned woman. The look in her eyes and her body language told it all.

She stood five feet three with long, slender fingers. Her cinnamon brown skin hue glistened with sweat. The woman had big beaded eyes that had dark circles underneath. Her skinny body frame was slumped as if she was high and drunk. The tangled black tresses, which looked like a wig, were a mess as it sat atop her head.

"Zabriah, I never did any of those things to you. I tried to be there for you," Jotson stated, slowly backing away from the woman who was coming towards him.

"My folks told you that if you didn't do right by me that you would no longer see the day of light. Well, guess what you and the bitch you spending it with has expired," she voiced in a deranged timbre.

At the same time Zabriah talked, I slowly reached into my purse and pulled out the chrome .22, which I took from Jonzella.

"Zabriah, take yo' crazy as ,' Jotson stated as the tear stained faced female brought forth a gun.

Fearing for the life of my unborn child and myself, I fired a direct shot into the bitch's chest. My breathing was erratic as lights began to flip on in people's homes. Voices started becoming clear as Jotson quickly turned around to face me. My body was shaking uncontrollably as I felt that I couldn't move.

Quickly snatching the gun out of my hand, he whispered, "I'm going to take this charge, if it is one. Call twelve right now. You will be a witness, and they will ask you questions. When they ask what happen, you will tell them that I shot her instead of you. Do you understand?"

"What if someone saw me shoot her instead of you?" I questioned lowly as I searched my small purse for my phone.

"It doesn't matter. I will take the rap for it," he voiced quickly before yelling for someone to call the police.

Quickly looking around the apartment complex, I didn't see anyone outside. Yet, I knew someone was looking. As I shook my head, I felt vomit rushing from the pit of my belly. Soon as I placed my hands over my mouth, a man from behind me asked what happened. Not able to hold the contents down, I vomited, all over my motherfucking shoes.

"I shot someone. Now, call the folks," Jotson said as he rubbed my back.

It wasn't long before we heard the sirens wailing.

"I guess someone called them the moment the gun went off," Jotson rapidly stated in my ear before continuing, "Don't forget that you are the witness. I shot her."

Nodding my head, I dry heaved for several more seconds before a cop car arrived. Once the cops stepped out of their squad car, I just knew that I was going to shit on myself. I hadn't been in a situation like this before, and I didn't know what to do or how to act normal. However, I wasn't feeling the fact that Jotson was going to take the charge of killing someone when he left his pistol on the damn table.

Jonzella, is going to curse my ass out something bad for taking her shit. Now, it's a body on her weapon. How in the hell am I going to tell her that I killed someone with her gun, and that someone else was taking the rap for my actions? I thought as the officers came towards Jotson and me.

CHAPTER 9
Jonzella

Saturday, February 25th

I had to stop worrying myself about Jonsey. She was a grown woman after all. I didn't like how she was alienating herself from me. We had never been this distant before; no matter what she was going through, I was there. Not one time had she been so closed in with me, and I really didn't like it. Over the past week, I talked to Jonsey twice and that was because she came to the house to retrieve some items. She hadn't been to work in God knows how long. Yep, I went to her place of employment. From my understanding, she had been deemed sick. I hoped like hell she had a doctor's excuse to cover her ass.

"Aye, babe, where your pistol at?" Totta asked as he put on his jeans.

"In the top drawer," I told him as I put clean sheets on the bed.

"It ain't in there."

"It gotta be. I don't go anywhere, so I didn't mess with it," I told him as I placed the fitted sheet at the top of the bed.

"A'ight, I'll look again," he replied as he walked towards the dresser.

As I proceeded to place another sheet on the bed, Totta informed me that the gun wasn't where I had put it. I stopped making up the bed to aid his ass in looking for my gun. Upon reaching my dresser, I pulled out my undergarments. Not one time did my hand run across my chrome pistol. With a frown on my face, I pondered where it could be.

"Told your ass it wasn't in there," Totta voiced in an agitated tone.

Shaking my head, I stopped searching the drawer and began thinking where I could've put it. While thinking of the last time I carried my pistol, I remembered putting it in the top drawer—where I always put it, underneath my panties and bras. Absolutely lost as to where my gun could be, I began searching every part of my room.

"How in the fuck you so careless with a gun, Jonzella?" Totta fussed while helping me look for it.

Getting angry, I yelped, "Dude, I wasn't careless with my shit. I put it where I always put it...in that damn top drawer."

"Well, it ain't there. You know once a month I clean that damn thing."

Sighing heavily, I wasn't in the mood to argue with him about a gun that I knew to put up. Twenty minutes later, I came to the realization that I didn't have possession of my gun.

Ambling towards the nightstand, I grabbed my phone. Dialing Jonsey's number, I prayed that she answered. As her phone rang, the front door opened, followed by being shut quickly.

"That gun is registered to you. You need to report it stolen. The last thing you want is for someone to put a body on that motherfucker, and you get held responsible for it, Jonzella. How in the hell could you be so careless as to not make sure that you had it?" Totta fussed.

"I told yo' black ass that I had put it up, damn it!"

Losing my mind about my weapon, Jonsey stepped in the room quietly.

I came to a complete stop when I saw my sister's scared, trembling body. Instantly, I stopped worrying about finding the gun and focused on my sister.

"Jonsey, what is wrong with you? What happened?" I questioned as I ambled towards her.

"I shot someone last night," she lightly voiced at the same time Totta's phone began to ring.

"What the hell? Why? Who?" I inquired as my eyes bucked.

"Was it with Jonzella's gun?" Totta asked right after I bombarded her with questions.

Totta ignored his phone, which pissed me off. The ringing of it had me wanting to bust it against the wall.

"Answer the damn phone, Totta!" I yelped, placing my eyes on him.

"Not until she answers those damn questions. I need to know how much control damage I gotta do for your sister's fuck up," he stated angrily as his phone stopped ringing, only to start back.

The phone stopped ringing seconds before Totta said, "Aye, Dank, I'mma call you b--."

"Jonsey, what happened?" I asked again as she took a seat at my study desk, followed by me kneeling in front of her.

"Mane, I know you lying!" Totta yelped in the phone.

"There was this female that threatened my life and the person that I was with. She pulled out a gun, and I pulled out yours. Before I knew it, I squeezed the trigger. I shot her in the chest. She died on the scene," my sister said as tears streamed down her face.

"Oh, God," I voiced while putting my arms around her shaking frame.

"Why you touched that gun in the first place, Jonsey? It wasn't yours!" Totta yelped, causing me to turn towards him with squinty eyes.

"Totta, calm down," I voiced through clenched teeth.

"Fuck that. I ain't finna have your sister fucking up our family because she made a stupid ass decision to take your gun and shoot somebody. The deceased bitch came after Jotson's ass."

Pulling away from Jonsey, I studied her wet, blank face. Before I could ask her was Totta's statement true, she began to sob that she was sorry, and that she was scared for her life since the female had threatened to end her life as well.

Sighing heavily, Totta asked, "Is it true that Jotson was arrested for the shooting?"

Nodding her head, Jonsey cried more.

Not understanding what in the hell was going on, I took a seat on my bed and demanded that Jonsey tell me everything. In ten minutes, Totta and I knew what took place and I wasn't going to lie and say I was upset with the choice that Jonsey made. If she hadn't taking my gun, I would've been burying her within the week.

"That gun is tied into Jonzella's name, Jonsey. Your boy ain't gonna be saved once they run the gun's number. So, if you think he's in the clear...you are sadly mistaken. I don't trust that nigga. So Jonzella, get your ass up and let's report the gun stolen."

"No, don't do that!" Jonsey screamed before bursting into tears.

"I don't have any other choice. I don't want any issues when it comes to the law with my gun being a murder weapon. I want to make sure that my name is in the clear. I don't know if I'll be able to carry another weapon legally."

"If things turn out for the worse, I don't want to go to prison for a murder," she sobbed.

"If it was self-defense, like you proclaimed, then you won't have any problems," Totta quickly hissed at her before looking at me and saying, "Get dressed. We finna go take care of this gun situation."

Nodding my head, I told Jonsey that I had to do it.

Skipping out of my room, Jonsey was in tears. Something in my core didn't feel right about reporting the gun stolen.

Turning to look at Totta, I said, "I'm not going to report the gun stolen. Jotson is taking the rap for the shooting. That would be a slap in the face if I did that. Let's just see how things work out. I refuse to throw him under the bus for what he's done. You can be mad or whatever. However, I'm going to act as if I still have my gun in the drawer and I suggest your ass do the same," I voiced sternly as I glared into my man's face before skipping off.

On the way out of the door, Totta's phone began to ring. At the same time, someone was knocking on the front door. As I slid down the hallway, I peeped into Jonsey's room. She was lying on the bed softly weeping. My heart went out to her as she was dealing with her first kill.

Knock. Knock. Knock.

"I'm coming," I stated loudly as I went to the front door.

"It's Dank, baby," Totta announced from behind me as I unlocked and opened the door.

Greeting my boyfriend's partner, I stepped onto the porch. As I observed the chilly, beautiful morning, I deeply inhaled the scent of the earth. It was refreshing. The street we lived on was quiet, just the way I liked. Old oak trees stood strong as the light wind ruffled the leaves on the weak branches. Birds were chirping a tune that I loved to hear. Zoning out and becoming one with the earth, I closed my eyes and continued breathing in and out. My one-on-one time with the earth was cut short when Dank began talking as he and Totta stepped onto the porch.

"So, the nigga's taking charge of what happened?" he asked Totta as my baby closed the front door.

"From what Jonsey said he is," Totta replied as I took a seat on the lounge chair.

"A'ight. Well, all I can tell you is be prepared for whatever happens. I don't know what angle this nigga Jotson hitting at, but I got my eyes on him," Dank voiced before slipping into the house.

Totta took a seat next to me, placing his eyes on me.

Sliding my hand into his, I said, "I'm ignorant on what can happen in a situation like this. What exactly are we looking at?"

"Truthfully?"

"Yes," I said as I nodded my head.

"There are four sets of fingerprints on that gun...yours, mine, Jotson, and Jonsey's. Once 12 run a check on the gun, your name will pop up in the system. Homicide detectives will be asking you questions pertaining to the gun. There will be an investigation into this murder until it's cleared off as self-defense. You and I will be cleared. Jonsey is the only one I'm not sure what will happen to, especially if they ask to speak with her sooner than later. The residue from the gun will be somewhere on her body and clothing since she is the one that fired the gun. If things go the way I hope, this shit will be over within six to eight months and deemed as a self-defense charge."

Dropping my head onto his shoulders, I said, "I need to go comfort my sister."

"They aren't arguing. Give them some time to get their shit together. Let's go for a walk," Totta voiced as he stood.

In need of getting away from the chaos, I did what he asked of me. The walk was well needed. It helped me take my mind away from the possibility of shit going south with my sister. I was able to focus on the little one I was carrying. It helped Totta and me figure out where we wanted to move; thus, I brought up that we need to stay at his place for a little while.

"I don't think we need to be away from Jonsey at the moment. She's not as strong as you. She has a conscious that makes me weak at times," he replied seriously as we turned around in the center of my neighborhood, aiming for my crib.

"Yeah, she's soft. So, are you okay with me not reporting the gun stolen?" I inquired while bringing his right hand to my lips.

"Yes, I am. I admire Jotson for what he did. Ain't too many niggas gonna take the rap for a murder charge for a broad much less one they hadn't smashed yet," he voiced, honestly.

"But why did Casey say something about keeping his eyes on Jotson?"

"Jotson is a master con artist. He's a sophisticated, calm, sweet-talking jackboy. He cons vulnerable females, and they don't see it coming until it's too late. That's what happened with the broad, Zabriah...the chick who Jonsey shot."

With bucked eyes, I stopped walking, followed by saying, "Explain."

"Jotson and Zabriah had been kicking it for three years, strong, might I add. He was caring and loving. Catering to her needs and being the man of the year. He acted as if he wanted to spend the rest of his life with her. Lil' nigga didn't entertain bitches or none of that fuck shit. Before you knew it, that nigga had access to her bank accounts. She was bought him a car, a nice startup kit of heroin to weed. She took care of that nigga. Zabriah was in love with that nigga. She proposed to him at the beginning of last year. He accepted it. Three months into their engagement, he started messing around with women who made more money than Zabriah. In June of last year, he broke the engagement off, but not before wiping Zabriah's two bank accounts clean. The dumb bitch had her trust fund in her savings account, which that nigga had access to. She went dumb behind the shit he did to her. I mean stone damn crazy. She started bucking every time she saw him. The shit got so bad that he had to put a restraining order--" my man explained before cutting his sentence off.

With a questionable facial expression, I glared at Totta. He didn't cut his sentence of for nothing. I had to know why he stopped talking upon the mention of a restraining order.

Shaking his head with a smile on his face, Totta chuckled, "That's one slick motherfucka!"

"What?" I asked in a puzzled timbre.

"He's going to get off on this charge. All because he put that paperwork on the broad. He's going to claim self-defense and get off."

Now, I was one worried motherfucker because that meant that bastard was going to con my sister into whatever he wanted her to do. That was a major issue for me! I swear it felt like I couldn't catch a damn break. First, it was Renee. Second, it was me trying to break free from Totta because he and Casey wanted my brothers dead. Then, I had to bury my brothers. Third, I had to deal with the knowledge that my father was a motherfucking gangster, whom had his sons killed. Now, I had to deal with unnecessary bullshit with a nigga that got a track record of conning vulnerable women.

I was not in the right mindset to be dealing with anything negative bullshit; yet, I had to find a way to make sure that Jonsey didn't fall down the rabbit hole.

Bringing me closer to him, Totta kissed me on the side of my cheek before saying, "Ahh, woman, don't you worry about a thing. Me and Dank gonna make sure everything go smoothly. I promise you that."

CHAPTER 10
Casey

Ever since I left Jonsey and Jonzella's crib late Saturday night, I tried wrapping my mind on why Jotson said that he killed a woman when he didn't. Then, it dawned on me that he would get off scoot free. Yet, who would want to go through all that legal shit when they didn't have to? Then, another thing dawned on me, he really liked Jonsey. I didn't understand how a person could like someone so early to the point they were willing to take a murder charge, even if they plead self-defense.

Ring. Ring. Ring.

Rolling over to retrieve my phone, I saw Danzo calling. Without a moment's hesitation, I answered the phone.

"Yo."

"Aye, man. I just got word from a little breezy that stay out there with Jotson that one of the elderly ladies that stay two doors down from him is running her mouth about what she saw. The elderly lady capping her mouth about who really shot Zabriah. According to the little breezy, the old hag cares dearly for Jotson," Danzo stated as he inhaled.

Sighing heavily while shaking my head, I sat upright in my lonely bed.

"I hate when people don't stay in their place," I replied, shaking my head.

"What are the odds she will go to twelve with her information?"

"Ain't no telling, mane. Ain't no damn telling," I told him as I lifted the black satin sheet off my body.

"Is there anything that you want me to do?"

"Have your little breezy politely tell that old hag to shut the fuck up and not repeat anything that she's been talking about," I voiced while descending the stairs.

"A'ight."

"Yeah," I replied before ending the call.

If that old bitch decided to open her damn mouth, then she was going to open some shit that she didn't have any business. She would be placing Jonsey in the building of someone's prison, which I wasn't hearing.

As soon as I approached the kitchen, I fixed myself a bowl of cereal, followed by dialing Totta's number. After seven rings, his answering machine picked up. Not leaving a message, I hung up, calling Jonsey next. On the fourth ring, she answered the phone.

"Hello," her groggy yet beautiful voice stated.

"Hey. You good?" I asked as I took a seat at the kitchen table.

"I think so," she replied.

"Aye, I just got word that an individual is talking about what they saw."

The line went silent.

"Did you hear me?" I inquired before shoveling a spoonful of Fruit Loops into my mouth.

"Yeah. What are they going to do?"

"The noisy person, or twelve?" I questioned to make sure that we were on the same page.

"The noisy person," her soft voice replied.

"I don't know yet. All I can say is that you need to be talking to Jotson. Y'all gotta be on one accord. However, if this investigation goes as I think it will...twelve, the prosecutor, DA, and the detectives are going to know that he didn't fire that gun."

"But he told them that he did do it," she stated before sighing.

"Jonsey, they aren't going to take his word for it. They will fully investigate things until it's completely solved. Why you think he's being charged with murder instead of self-defense? They have to prove it, not just go on his word."

"Wait...did you say murder?"

"Yes."

"Oh, my God," she whined. "IIow long will this investigation go on?"

"Who knows."

The line went silent for several brief seconds before Jonsey told me that she would talk to me later. After ending the call, I shook my head while sighing sharply. I hoped that all this shit she was involved in would disappear soon. I prayed that she wouldn't spend a day in nobody's jail or prison.

That was when an idea flashed in my brain. Quickly gobbling down my cereal, I had to handle some important business, and it couldn't wait a second longer. After taking a short shower, I dressed in casual clothing and aimed for the city jail. I had to chat with Jotson myself, on a coded tip—of course.

An hour and forty minutes later, Jotson was strolling through a dingy beige door. With a shocked facial expression spread across his light-skinned, thin face, he nodded at me. Once the guards unshackled his hands, Jotson took a seat across from me.

"What do I owe the pleasure of seeing you, Dank?" Jotson asked with a straight face.

"I needed to know how you are holding up."

"I'm good, and you?" he replied with a smirk on his face.

"A'ight. Is there anything that I can do for you?"

"Nope."

"Are you sure?"

"Yep."

Silence overcame us as I wanted to know the latest information on his case. There was no other way to say what I wanted to know; thus, I jumped right in.

"What type of time are you looking at? How's the investigation going? Have you talked to Jonsey?" I fired off as I held his eye contact.

Nodding his head, Jotson replied calmly, "So, *you* are the father of her child, huh?"

"I am," I replied as I noticed that he wasn't pleased with my answer.

"So, that's why you are here, huh?" he chuckled lightly.

As I nodded my head, I didn't utter a word.

"Well, well, well. I got your nuts in a choke hold if I don't do what I originally set out to do, huh?"

Ah, there is that Jotson that I've had the pleasure of not, the con-artist, I thought as I glared at the nigga.

"So, you want to know how much time I'm looking at, how's the investigation going, and have I talked to Jonsey, huh?"

"Yep," I replied, rapidly.

"Well, since we righteously don't fuck with each other...let's just say this can go one of two ways," he laughed for a brief time before continuing, "I can have all this shit dismissed within the next twenty-four hours, or I can go on with my decision of what I originally stated."

Seeing that he was putting stipulations on shit, I leaned forward and spat, "What are you saying, my nigga?"

"If I had known that you was smashing, I would've let her pregnant ass drown," he replied with a snarl.

Shaking my head, the feud between Jotson and I was real.

While I looked at the foolish ass young nigga, I couldn't believe that he was going to make a demand just to continue saving Jonsey's ass. While we glared at each other, the hatred in his eyes for me was real. In reality, the shit was silly as hell.

"What are you willing to do to keep me on the same path that I am on?" he voiced, interrupting my thoughts.

Not flinching, I asked, "What do you want?"

Before standing the fuck nigga said, "Every damn thing out of your six savings accounts, or I'm telling the truth. You got six hours to find a way to communicate yes or no."

As the guard took his funky ass away, I exited the visitation area with one person on my mind, J-Money. There was no way in hell I was going to pay the fuck nigga. He was good as dead to me. That little runt was pissed at me for something that wasn't my fault to begin with—one of his ex-bitches jumping on my dick, all the while displaying and screaming that she was team Dank.

Soon as the bright sun hit my black face, I was anxious to get in my car. Once I did, I started the engine as I dialed J-Money's number. On the seventh ring, he answered the phone.

"Speak to me," he voiced as he inhaled deeply.

"You at the crib?" I inquired as I left the city jail's parking lot.

"Nawl, but I will be in about three hours or so."

"Soon as you touch down, I need to holla at cha," I stated.

"A'ight. I'll call you soon as I touch in the city."

"Bet," I replied before we ended the call.

Zooming to the ladies' crib, I was content knowing Jotson was going to be dead soon. The way The Savage Clique was setup, they had pull and could do anything anyone asked of them. A simple homicide in a jail was nothing for them to do. However, I would have to do a lot of shit for them in return, which I was more than willing to do.

Pulling into the grassy parking lot, I saw Jonsey sitting on the porch, wrapped in a thick, pink, green, and white floral blanket. Shutting off the engine, I exited my vehicle. Scrolling towards the porch, I noticed that she was in deep thought.

"Hey," my thick voiced announced as I took a seat next to her.

"Hi," she replied, placing her glossy eyes on me.

"I want you to know that you will be okay. There will be no investigation, or none of that shit."

As she opened her mouth, I shook my head before saying, "Don't ask me any questions. I just need you to know that you will be okay."

Nodding her head, Jonsey placed her head on my shoulder. Placing a kiss on her forehead, I she cooed. She snuggled closer to me, bringing a huge grin to my face. Jonsey was all that I wanted, and I had to get her to see that. I was nothing without her.

As we were quiet, I heavily enjoyed the bright shining sun as the wind blew lightly; I chuckled at a group of chirping birds as they fought over bread crumbs. Sitting on the porch with my lady in the crook of my arm, I was in a calm place. God knows I wouldn't be the moment I tell J-Money what I need from The Savage Clique.

"I think we should go inside. It's too chilly for me, and I'm getting sleepy," she voiced, breaking the silence.

"Okay," I replied as I grabbed her hands, leading us into the warm front room.

I loved the smelled of the ladies' home; it smelled sweet and clean. There hasn't been one time that I'd been at their living quarters, and it was nasty and stinky. They never left dishes in the sink, on the stove, or around the house. I had to say that they were extremely clean women.

The closing of the Jonsey's bedroom door brought me out of my observance zone. Kicking off my shoes and placing them beside the door, I glanced at my lady as she crawled across her bed. Removing my shirt, I neatly placed it on top of her dresser. Ambling towards the bed, I realized how much I cared for her. I knew that an apology was in store for my behavior towards her.

Softly planting my body underneath the purple, gray, and pink bedding covers, I placed my eyes on Jonsey and said, "The other day I was out of line, and I'm sorry for how I tried to handle you."

Biting down on her lip, Jonsey calmly said, "I forgive you, Casey. Don't test me like that again. Next time, you might get what you are seeking."

***

"Aye, you must've touched down…since I got a missed call from you," I told J-Money while yawning.

"Shit, yeah. I'm out and about. Nigga, it's after two. Why in the hell you sleeping in so damn late?"

"You know how it is when you get a woman pregnant. Shit, you get some of them symptoms she has," I chuckled as I felt Jonsey stirring.

"Null, nih!" He laughed before continuing, "Welcome to fatherhood, my nigga. Congratulations."

"Thank you."

"No problem. So, when you trying to meet up?"

"Soon as possible. Scratch that, I need at least thirty minutes to fully wake up. Tell me what time is good for you?" I stated, stretching.

"How 'bout 3 at Legion's crib, woe?"

Knowing that Legion was good people, I replied, "That's cool. I hope she don' baked some pies and cakes. A nigga need 'bout ten of those mini sweet potato pies."

"That's what her crazy ass doing now," J-Money voiced.

"Bet dat shit. In that case, I'mma get my ass up and move around. I'll see you in a minute."

"A'ight."

Ending the call, I looked at Jonsey, whom was staring at me.

"What?" I inquired while pulling her close to me.

"What are we going to do about the pregnancy?"

"I want to be a daddy. What about you?" I voiced gently, rubbing her face.

"I don't know."

"Well, you need to heavily think about it. I'm not going to act like I'm cool with you having an abortion because I'm not. I want you to be on the same page as me. I want us to be a family."

"Are you sure that's what you want?"

"Yes," I replied, truthfully.

"Okay. I just need to make sure that's what I--," she stated before throwing her hands over her mouth as she fled the bed. I knew what time it was; thus, I didn't say anything.

While she was in the bathroom vomiting, Totta yelled, "Shit, Jonzella. Oh, God! Mane, I'mma be sick as hell! Take that shit to the bathroom! You need to keep a trash can in this room!"

Her bedroom door opened; he rapidly walked down the hall as Jonzella twisted the bathroom's doorknob.

"You might want to run to the kitchen, your sister bent over the toilet," I voiced, two seconds too late.

As my eyes were glued on the scene in the bathroom, I had a frown on my face. The retching noises from the ladies turned my damn stomach upside down. Jonsey was kneeling in front of the toilet as Jonzella threw up in the trash can. I felt the urge to vomit as I hopped to my feet to put on my clothes and shoes.

"Dank, mane, shit real up in this motherfucka," Totta stated as I exited Jonsey's room.

"Hell yeah. My stomach ain't built for this shit, woe."

"Mine ain't either," he informed me before walking off.

"Aye, I'm finna meet up with J-Money. You rolling?" I yelled as Totta entered Jonzella's room.

"Yeah. Let me make sure she's alright before I leave," he replied.

"A'ight."

At two forty-five p.m., we were heading away from Lee Oaks. We were confident the women would be okay until we returned. They were snuggled in bed with a bottle of Ginger-Ale, a pack of crackers, and a medium-sized waste basket beside the bed.

"What's this meeting about?" Totta inquired as I pulled into Legion's front yard.

"Me having Jotson killed tonight."

Taken aback by my comment, Totta said, "Explain, nigga."

I gave him the rundown on the conversation I had with Jotson.

By the time I was done, Totta replied, "Yeah, he needs to be knocked off the map. You do know the consequences of asking such a favor, right?"

"Yep, and I'm willing to do whatever his boss lady say to have that fuck nigga murked as soon as the evening meal is passed out," I replied before exiting my vehicle. Totta stepped out of the car as well.

J-Money met us soon as I placed my right foot on the clean porch.

Dapping us up, he greeted us with a, "What's good?"

"Shid...a favor for a favor," I replied, getting straight to the point.

"Talk to me," he probed as he lit a Newport.

"Jotson...dead...at six," I voiced while glaring at him.

Nodding his head, J-Money pulled out his cell phone. He pressed a lone number before bringing the phone to his ear.

Several seconds later, he said, "Chief, are you in the city?"

For a favor of my caliber, J-Money had to call X, who him and the other niggas called Chief. It was protocol. She was the only one that could approve a hit of this magnitude.

"I need you at Legion's crib," J-Money voiced.

Apparently, X must've said okay because of J-Money's response was 'a'ight'.

After putting his mobile device in the gold holster, J-Money looked at me and said, "Chief on the way. She said she's ten minutes out."

"Cool," I replied as Totta nodded his head.

A different topic took place until we heard speakers knocking loudly. With a smile on my face, I knew that X was close by.

"The Boss" by Rick Ross was blasting nearby. No one in the city was beating hard as X. She loved all songs that had to do with bosses. Hell, she was the head honcho in charge, damn near throughout the country!

"Ooooou, that's my baby coming through," Legion stated as she sashayed her thick behind out of the front door.

"You bet not call her that. She ain't with that shit, Legion," J-Money said in an aggressive manner while looking at her.

She smacked her lips and rolled her eyes. While waiting to get a glimpse of X, Legion chopped it up with us. That woman had a mean crush on X, and no one could stop how she felt about the gorgeous Queenpin.

The music grew louder while X's black on black, trimmed in gold 1976 Chevy Caprice crept down the road. On some G-shit, she stayed on! Didn't fear no one; she didn't! Ready to put a hole in anybody, she was! She made majority of us hood niggas look pie as fuck.

I had never seen a woman so tactful every time I saw her. She ran a secure organization, and she was fucking untouchable. How in the hell she pulled it off? I had no damn idea.

Turning the music down, X parked on the curb. Totta, J-Money, and I waltzed towards The Beast while Legion stayed on the porch. The moment X stepped onto the curb, Legion became a fucking cheerleader, yelling hey. X spoke and placed her eyes on us.

"What's up, X," Totta and I stated in unison.

"Coolin'. What's good fellas?" she inquired while looking between Totta and me.

"I need Jotson knocked off," I replied in a low timbre.

"He still in jail, right?" she inquired before firing up a Newport.

"Yes."

"What time you want him dead?" she asked as she pulled out a small, black flip phone, all the while looking me in the eyes.

"By 6."

With a blank facial expression, she voiced in a boss-like manner, "A'ight. Now, that that is out of the way. Here's what I need for you to do for me. I need you to show these little niggas how to properly respect the dope game and everything that goes along with it. I need them to learn that once you catch a sell case that they need to shut the fuck up and do their bid. They are starting to compromise what I have built. I really don't want to have half of these young niggas missing and found years later. Can you do that for me, Dank?"

Knowing that was a hard task, I had no choice but to accept.

Nodding my head, I replied, "Yes."

"Cool. I'll have your favor done at the requested time. That's all y'all need?" she asked while looking at each of us.

J-Money said, "Yes, Chief."

Totta and I said, "Yes."

"Very well, then y'all have a great day."

"Same to you," we replied before she brought The Beast to life.

We didn't say a word as she boomed and zoomed down the road.

Standing on the edge of the curb, J-Money looked at me and said, "Woe, you do know you might have to murk at least fifteen of them young niggas?"

"Yep," I replied.

"A'ight. The West and The Nawf are where the issues lie."

"A'ight," I replied as I dapped him up before leaving.

On the way to scope the young ones out on the Westside, I sighed heavily as I didn't know the right way of going about my task. I had several thoughts of how to get them in compliance; yet, I didn't know how it would turn out. So, the best conclusion that I came up with was to watch them for four days then drop down on their asses.

Interrupting my thoughts Totta announced, "We always been in some shit together, and we in this here together. Yeah, you doing this for Jonsey; yet, I gotta help you because of Jonzella. If anything happens to Jonsey, she is going to lose her damn mind, and I can't have that. So, whatever we gotta do, we gonna do it. If we gotta bury half of these young niggas to get them on board when it comes down to that snitching shit, then fuck it, we gotta do it."

Chapter 11
Jonsey

Friday, March 3rd

Morning sickness wasn't doing me so badly today; however, Jonzella was receiving the worst end of it. I tried my best to be there for her, but she was making my stomach weak. I didn't do well with other folks vomiting. I kept her stocked with water, ginger-ale, and crackers. It seemed as if they weren't working for her. I prayed that she would find some relief soon.

Deciding not to sit in the house today, I quickly decided that I would get out and enjoy the day. I had two more days to enjoy my non-working life before I went back to the hellhole of Wal-Mart and their customers. I wasn't feeling school at the moment; thus, I didn't want to go. I was glad when summer break finally arrived.

After I was dressed, I told Jonzella that I was heading out for a bit.

Nodding her head, she said, "Be careful."

"Always," I replied after placing a kiss on her forehead.

"Hey," she called out as I reached the threshold of her door.

Turning around to face her, I replied, "Yeah."

"How's things going with Jotson?"

"I don't know. He hadn't called me since Tuesday morning."

"Do you think he's going to continue saying that he's the shooter?"

"Yes. I don't see why he would recant now."

"Okay. Well, enjoy your day."

"I will do."

Skipping out of the house, Jonzella had me thinking about Jotson. It was odd that I hadn't talked to him since Tuesday morning. I wanted to know how things were going, and if he needed anything. After all, I had to make sure that he at least wasn't hurting for anything.

After I started the engine, I took a seat in my car.

Pulling out my phone, I Googled the city's jail number. Upon receiving the number,. The phone began ringing. I was a nervous mess as I didn't know what to say or how to say it, but I needed someone to tell Jotson to call me. Within five minutes a raspy voiced man answered the phone.

"Hi, I'm trying to deliver a message to an inmate. How do I go about doing that?" I inquired.

"Is it an emergency?" the man inquired.

Lying my tail off, I replied, "Yes."

He asked me what the inmate name was and I told him.

"Umm, ma'am, I'm sorry I can't relay that message."

Shocked, I stated, "May I ask why not?"

Sighing heavily, he replied, "I'm not at liberty to say."

Furious with him not being able to pass a simple message, I ended the call without saying so much as goodbye or have a nice day.

Reversing my vehicle from the grassy driveway, I couldn't think of a reason why Jotson wasn't calling me or why the individual that answered the phone couldn't relay a message. Curiosity got the best of me as I thought of many reasons. In a short time, I had several negative thoughts, which scared me.

What if he's told them the truth? Will they be coming after me? Why would he say he'll take the charge if he intended on not upholding his end? I thought as I fled off my street.

I was supposed to have been enjoying my day; yet, I couldn't because I was thinking about being in prison away from my child. Catching on to what I said, I realized that I wanted to keep the baby.

Quickly rerouting my destination, I placed my car in the back parking lot of Cope. As I strolled along the nicely decorated path towards the front of the building, I was anxious to get inside away from the displeasures of Jack Frost. The brisk wind was blowing harshly as the sun shined brightly. I wasn't built for the cold; I didn't care how many layers of clothes were piled onto my body.

Planting my feet on the steps, I ambled towards the front door. Opening it, I saw that the reception area was filled with women of all shapes and hues. The lovely tall woman greeted me as I greeted her. After signing in, I took a seat.

Twenty minutes passed before my name was called. I chatted with an older looking lady for ten minutes before she gave me the paperwork to take to the local Medicaid office.

Leaving the pregnancy resource center, I was okay with knowing that I made the right decision to continue my pregnancy. Placing my body in the cold cushion of my car, I started the engine and called Casey. On the second ring, he answered.

"Hello," his thick, sexy voice stated.

"Hi. Did I wake you?"

"Yes, but it's okay. You okay?" he inquired before yawning.

"Yes, I'm fine. I just left Cope."

"What did they say?"

"I'm nine weeks and two days. The baby's estimated due date is October fourth."

"So, we have a fall baby, huh?" he asked excitedly, which caused me to smile.

"Yes, we do."

"What are you getting ready to do next?"

"I'm headed to DHR."

"Before you go there, stop by here. I want to go with you."

Smiling, I replied, "Are you sure? I don't know how long I'll be there."

"I'm going to be involved every step of the way. Do you understand me?"

"Yes."

"Now, that we got that out of the way I'll leave the door unlocked, come on in."

"K," I replied as I reversed my car.

"Have you ate, yet?"

"Not really hungry. Don't want anything to upset this little creature."

"Well, I'm starving. We gotta go somewhere and get some food."

"Okay."

"Well, I'm finna go jump in the shower."

"A'ight, sir. End the call, please," I giggled.

Three minutes later, the call ended. I zoomed towards my child's father crib. One thing I better not have to encounter with him today is one of his bitches coming for me. I will not be dealing with the foolishness.

Six minutes later, I was parking my car behind Casey's turquoise Infiniti. Not wasting anytime hopping out of my car, I did so as if a fire was set under my ass. Once inside of his home, I informed him that I was there. The moment he placed his eyes on me, Casey's dick was on brick mode. He was pressing the issue for me to join him, which I didn't. I was on a mission, and it surely wasn't a dick one. As I exited his bathroom, my child's father chocolate ass was fussing about having a massive hard on.

Shaking my head while laughing, I yelled, "Hurry up. I might give you some cat when we get back."

After thirty minutes, his black ass was gliding down the steps with a huge smile on his face. Hopping to my feet, I zoomed towards the door before he tried to corner me on the sofa. His sexy ass wasn't getting any until we handled business with our unborn child.

"Aye, I'm driving," he stated as he closed the door behind him.

"My car or yours?"

"Since, your car is behind mine. We are going in yours," he replied, placing a kiss on the back of my neck.

Slipping into the passenger seat of my car, I exhaled. I was tired of driving. For once, I was able to relax in the passenger seat like a spoiled queen. That was, until that black bastard reversed my car. Instantly, I was crazy as hell for letting him drive. I forgot that he drove like a bat out of hell. My poor toes were balled as I was snuggled against the seatbelt, which was starting to irritate my neck.

Coming to my senses, I said, "I'm not trying to die, Casey. I don't have an appointment, you know."

"I'm not driving that bad," he replied, chuckling.

"Whatever," I replied, rolling my eyes.

We chatted lightly until we made it to our destination. As soon as he parked the car, I saw the bitch that came over to his house some days ago. Placing her eyes on us, she had a nasty glare on her face.

"You better not do or say shit out of the way," he commanded while grabbing my hand.

"If the frog leaps, she will get smashed."

***

"Damn, you were really hungry, huh?" I asked Casey as he smashed his T-bone steak.

Chuckling, he spat, "I'm always hungry. Been this way since I can remember."

"You aren't feeling sick, are you?" he inquired as he placed his utensils on the cleaned, white plate.

"No. Just don't have an appetite."

"Your body needs the nutrients. Just try the salad, baby."

Opening my mouth to speak, a sound didn't come out because of what I overhead.

"Don't nobody know who killed Jotson. Only thing being said is that his neck was broken," a female to the right of us stated.

Instantly, I felt sad.

"Damn, that's fucked up. He was fine as fuck though," the broad across the table replied to her friend.

Placing my eyes on Casey, he glared into my face. An eerie feeling overcame me as I observed his appearance. I studied him for a long time so I didn't hear the waitress talking to us.

"Jonsey," Casey called out, snapping me into reality.

"Yeah," I replied.

"Do you want a to-go box?" he asked as the waitress looked at me,

"Yes please."

Nodding her head she said, "Sure thing."

I couldn't wait until we left the restaurant; I had to know did Casey have Jotson killed. It seemed as if the waitress took her damn time coming back with the to-go box and the ticket. When she arrived, I was antsy to arrive at my car. Neither of us said a word until we were safely inside of my car.

"Why did you look at me like that once you heard Jotson was dead?" he inquired while placing the gearshift in reverse.

"Did you have anything to do with it?"

Without a moment's hesitation, Casey calmly replied, "Yes, and I will do it again if the fuck nigga could come back."

Silence overcame me as I glared at him. There were so many questions as to why; yet, I felt that I didn't need to know. My day was going great, and I wasn't going to ruin it by asking him why he had Jotson killed.

As he drove away from the restaurant, Casey asked, "Do you want to know why I had him killed?"

"Not really. Don't want to get upset when I'm having a great day."

"You will ask me once it hits you that I had him killed, so I'm going to get it out of the way," he voiced seriously before continuing. "Once he found out that you were pregnant by me, he tried to extort me by saying that I had a certain amount of time to say yes or no before he told the truth on what happened to Zabriah. Not the one to have you in any type of trouble, I took it upon myself to get the nigga off this Earth."

I had nothing to say, so I remained quiet. I was in complete shock that Jotson would say what he told Casey. I didn't want to believe Casey; yet, I knew that he wouldn't lie to me. All sorts of questions consumed my mind, causing me to become a ball of confusion.

"Talk to me, baby. What are you thinking? How are you feeling about the situation?" he questioned while grabbing my hand.

Shrugging my shoulders, I replied, "I'm confused as hell right now. I just have all these questions. I guess I'm not understanding why he would say and do all those sweet things, and then try to extort you upon learning that you are responsible for me being pregnant. Shit doesn't make any sense to me, Casey."

"It's simple, baby. That nigga is a con artist. Excuse me...he was a con artist."

As I shook my head, Casey drove from the restaurant as we didn't say another word. Yet, I couldn't stop asking myself questions.

Why did Jotson react in such a way to the knowledge of Casey being my child's father? What type of history did the two have? Was I a target for Jotson all along? Will there be others trying to come after me to get to Casey?

Those same questions never stopped being on my mind, even when we made it back to his house. While my body was responding to him in a sexual way, the questions were there. When he slid my clothes over my head, planting kisses all over my body while fingering me, those damn questions never left. The moment he began dicking me down, those questions ceased and didn't return. I accepted the fact that Casey wasn't going anywhere, and that not a soul was going to fuck with me or our family!

Caught Up In A D-Boy's Illest Love 3

Chapter 12
Totta

With the news of that fucker Jotson dead, I knew that I could breathe easy. I knew that he would not bring any stress to my homie or my girl anymore. Yeah, I cared about Jonsey, but my heart laid with the woman that I got pregnant. Seeing that it was time to celebrate before Dank and I had to hit the streets heavy to get those young niggas in check, I decided that I wanted to kick my Friday off the right way—all the way in some pregnant pussy, followed by going out to eat.

Jonzella and I debated over what restaurant was going to get my money. It was a battle between us. She wanted to go to Chili's because they didn't have food smells that would make her throw up. I wanted Mexican food, which upset her stomach. I was thankful that she stopped vomiting so much and looking poor-faced. I didn't understand morning sickness at all. I didn't know why it wasn't called anytime sickness, since that was what it really was.

"Mmm, this is really delicious," she voiced as she devoured the last of her chef's salad.

"I'm glad you are able to enjoy, woman. All that throwing up you was doing did a number on me. Are you sure you will be able to hold that salad down?" I asked as I cut into my steak smothered in mozzarella and parmesan cheese.

"I hope so. I'm going to take a salad home. I see that heavy food isn't for me. When we leave here, we need to go to Wal-Mart so that I can get some soft foods."

"Okay."

My eyes drifted to the left the moment I saw those funky ass detectives whom questioned me about Erica's ass. I wondered whether they were following me.

Catching the eye of our waitress, I motioned for her to come to our table.

While skipping her smiley ass towards the table, she was stopped by a family of six.

As I grunted loudly, Jonzella looked at me before asking, "What's wrong?"

"We need to blow this place. Detectives not too far from us," I stated lowly as our waitress finally sauntered away from the family of six.

When she approached the table, I rapidly stated, "We need our drinks and another Chef's salad to go and the ticket please."

"Sure thing. I will be back shortly," she replied with a bubbly attitude before walking away.

"Totta, don't you think it will look suspicious with you leaving just because they are here?" Jonzella asked as she shoveled three croutons in her mouth.

"Nope. I don't want to be anywhere near those fuckers. You know I don't like twelve."

In ten minutes, the waitress arrived with the check and the requested items. Giving her a fifty-dollar bill, I told her to keep the change. With a gracious smile on her face, she thanked us and told us to have a nice day.

On the way out of the door, one of the detectives rushed behind us.

"Joshua "Totta" Nixon, you aren't planning on skipping town, are you?" his ugly ass asked with food spilling from his mouth.

"Lawyer," I stated in a boss-like manner before escorting my lady out of the establishment.

Instantly, he left me the fuck alone. There was nothing else left to be said. I was very sure that poor ass detective didn't want the heat brought down on him. On the other hand, maybe that was what I needed to put under his ass.

As soon as I plopped my ass in the driver's seat, I retrieved my cell phone. Dialing my lawyer's number, I reversed my lady's car. The moment he answered the phone, I told him what was going on. Once I was done, he said the one statement that I wanted to hear. Ending the call, I had a huge smile on my face.

"Why are you smiling like a Cheshire cat?" Jonzella inquired as she connected her hand into mine.

"Because I just placed some heat on those damn detectives. I bet they asses won't be in my damn face unless they have some real fucking evidence."

"How is the case going anyway?"

"I have no idea, but I know one thing...they can't fuck with the kid because it's a bunch of heresy."

"You better make sure that they don't come for you. If you need to do a little more killing...then you need to take care of that shit. Our child and I need you, for life...in our lives," she replied soothingly as her eyes were glued to me.

With a smile on my face, I honestly replied, "I love you, girl."

"I love you more."

Ring. Ring. Ring.

Picking up my phone, I saw that it was Danzo calling. Swiping my hand to the left, I said hello before I placed the phone to my ear.

"Woe, where you at?"

"Shid, leaving the Eastside with my lady."

"A'ight. Come by when you get some free time."

Knowing that he had to relay a message, I replied with, "A'ight. Give me about forty-five minutes and I'll be pulling up."

"Okay den."

"Business calls?" Jonzella inquired as her cell phone rang.

"Yes, ma'am. Are you upset?" I asked, aiming for the interstate.

"No. You just make sure that you don't get into no more trouble."

"Yes, Captain," I chuckled as I squeezed her hand.

Fifteen minutes later, I pulled into the grassy driveway of the ladies duplex. I wasn't trying to be gone too long; thus, I told her so. Once I saw that she was comfortably sitting on the sofa, I exited their cozy home. As I hopped in my ride, I called Danzo.

"Yo'," he answered, on the first ring.

"I'm on the way," I stated as I heard a lot of background noise.

"Damn, you having a party ain't it?"

"Nawl, J-Money and Dank over here. You know them niggas love getting their asses whooped in this basketball game," he stated as I heard Dank yelling.

"Shid, we bettin' or what?"

"Mane, you know we stay betting, nigga. What kind of question is that?" Danzo laughed.

"Bet. I'll be pulling up soon. Tell them niggas to get their money ready."

"Aight."

With the call ended, I zoomed to one of the realest niggas crib that I knew besides The Savage Clique and Dank.

When we were younger, Marshall "Danzo" Lucas, Dank, and I hung together, off and on, during spring break and the summers. In the beginning, it was mostly Dank and I. All that changed the summer, Dank got punched in the face by Danzo's sister. Ever since then, when you saw one, you saw all of us. After the breaks, Dank went back home, Texas. My main partner was gone, and I was thrown off; so, Danzo and I became cool, but not as cool as me and Dank.

That character, Danzo, hung around some niggas I knew were flaw. I didn't need them around me, knowing my business; thus, I made sure Danzo knew I wasn't feeling the others he hung around.

Halfway into our junior year of high school, Danzo was banging heavily with those niggas. I didn't waste no time getting away from him. I kept shit cordial, but it was no hanging out type of shit. I didn't trust him until he showed me that he could be trusted. The day came when Danzo and those niggas fell out. Not one time did he chump them niggas out or talked shit about them. He acted as if he never hung around them. That's when I knew Danzo could be trusted; yet, I kept a close eye on him—all because of his background with those niggas.

My thoughts ceased the moment I parked behind Dank's whip.

Hopping out, I rushed inside to get a turn at whooping the fellas behind in the basketball game.

"Ohh, shit, here comes that shit talking ass nigga Totta," J-Money's gorgeous girlfriend stated before laughing.

"Simone, why you gotta do me like that?" I joked as I gave her a hug.

"Because, nigga, you are the king of talking shit," J-Money and Danzo stated in unison before laughing.

Looking around for Dank, I found his ass at the counter stuffing his face.

Shaking my head, I yelped, "Mane, every time I see yo' black ass you eating. Damn, dude, you be acting like you are hungry all the time."

"Shid, I do," he stated before laughing.

Taking a seat next to J-Money, I replied, "Shit don't make no sense."

Normal conversation took place until Ruger cleared his throat. Immediately, the game was shut off. J-Money told Danzo that he would holler at him later.

The look on his face told me that he wanted to know why he had to leave. On the verge of protesting, Danzo chose to leave versus to asking why he had to go--that was his best move. I guess the shaking of my head told him that it was best for him to leave. The last thing I needed was for him to fuck up our alliance with The Savage Clique.

Once Danzo left, we walked out of the back door. As soon as the screen door closed DB and Ruger started talking.

"Chief has called a meeting tonight at eleven at Safe House Eleven. The details of the meeting, I don't know. I know that all of us must be in attendance, including Dank."

"I'll be in attendance as well," I told him while briefly looking each of them in the face.

"She didn't say anything about you," Ruger stated with a raised eyebrow.

"Well, I guess you better be calling and informing her that I will be in attendance tonight," I told him while glaring into his blackened face.

Angrily clearing his throat and pulling his phone from the holster, Ruger aggressively pressed a single number. Placing the phone to his ear, he gave me a nasty stare.

Instantly, I began to chuckle and so did everybody else.

"Chief..." he stated while walking away from us.

"He's very protective of X," Dank spat in a joking manner.

"You have no idea just how overprotective he is of her," Rondon stated as he fired up a Newport.

Shortly afterwards, Ruger was strolling towards us. We waited on the response from their Chief.

"She said you can come," he stated lowly.

Rondon, Silky Snake, DB, Baked, and J-Money burst out in laughter.

Dank and I looked at them as if they were crazy. Apparently, there was an inside joke somewhere; thus, I had to know.

"What's so funny?" I inquired as I looked at the fellas.

"You'll learn soon...real soon," DB replied while chuckling.

Not knowing what in the hell they were talking about, I shrugged my shoulders.

"As protocol goes, y'all will have to ride with one of us," Silky Snake voiced while pulling a blunt from behind his ear.

"A'ight. Where we meeting up at?" Dank inquired.

"Be here at nine twenty-five," J-Money inquired.

With a frown on my face, I said, "I thought the meeting was to start at eleven."

"It is, but shid, we gotta drive to the country. Damn near going to Tuscaloosa," J-Money voiced.

"Oh, shit. Well damn...let me go put baby mama to sleep until I get back then," I chuckled as the fellas did as well.

"Congratulations on the new addition, my nigga," Baked stated as the others, minus Ruger, fell in line with the congratulations.

"Thanks."

"Is there anything that we need to know prior to this meeting?" Dank asked.

"Yeah, don't fuck over my Chief," Ruger spat.

"You don't have to worry about that, mane," Dank replied as I had several things I wanted to say to the ancient black nigga.

"Well, this pre-meeting is over with. Don't forget; be here at nine twenty-five. We are leaving promptly at nine-thirty," J-Money stated while tugging on the blunt.

"Bet," Dank and I replied in unison.

***

The ride to Safe House Eleven, aka S.H.E., was so far in the country that I wanted to tell them to turn around and take me the fuck back to The Gump. I thought I would never see houses or stores again. The entire ride was eerie as fuck. I kept my burner close by and off safety. Never knew what these niggas had on their minds. I wasn't as cool with them as Dank was.

I know damn well this ain't no fucking safe house, I thought as we pulled into a nice, single family home.

With a confused facial expression as I opened the back door, I said, "Mane, this is S.H.E.? Can't be."

Laughing, Rondon replied, "You better believe it."

"Well, damn. How sophisticated," I stated casually as Dank and I followed behind the fellas.

When we stepped onto the porch, X unlocked the screen door. She was one sexy ass broad. Normally, she had her hair braided into medium-sized box braids, but tonight she had her naturally, long hair hanging down. She was dressed in all-black, of course. A sports bra, tight fitted jogging pants, socks, and Nike sliders.

"Welcome, fellas. Have a seat, please."

Doing as she instructed, we placed our asses into the plush cushions of the sofa set, well minus Baked. His ass waltzed straight into the kitchen.

"How are y'all tonight?" she asked as she took a seat on the long, black sofa while glaring at Baked.

"Well. How about you?" Dank and I asked in unison as the other said, "Good, Chief."

"I'm Gucci," she replied as she took a sip from a wine glass.

Her eyes were glued on Baked, who was rummaging through the refrigerator.

"No matter how many times you eat nigga, yo' ass always rambling in the damn 'fridge," DB joked as the others said, "Hell yeah."

Ignoring his crew members, Baked stuffed several green grapes in his mouth before saying, "Chief?"

"Yeah."

"You got all this fruit in here and ain't ate shit. Let a brother take some to the crib," he voiced.

"You must be planning on cooking tomorrow?" she laughed.

"That's in the plans. You got a special request?" he replied, closing the refrigerator.

At once, The Savage Clique piped in orders. It was as if the nigga Baked was a damn chef by the way they rattled foods off that they wanted him to cook.

Cutting the requests short, he said, "Aye, nih, I'm only going to prepare two dishes each of you niggas want. Nothing more. Chief, you can get more."

"Yeah, you can take some fruit to the crib. What are you going to do with it?" she inquired, chuckling.

"Remember that fruit pie we were looking at on the food channel last night?" he asked her while walking into the front room.

"Hell yes!" she responded, excitedly.

"I'm going to make it," he announced as he took a seat beside her.

"I want them in mini pie form with the graham cracker crust in the bottom."

"I gotcha, Chief," he replied quickly.

"We will talk about that once we are done with this lil' meeting," she voiced to him before getting into boss mode.

"Totta, what is the reason you wanted to be in attendance tonight?" she questioned me as she placed her pretty brown eyes on me.

"Dank and I are partners. Whatever he has to do, so do I."

With a smile on her face, X nodded her head and said, "I love the bond y'all have."

"Thank you," Dank and I replied.

"I won't keep y'all long. I have added a little something else to the task. I want you to make those little runts feel the consequences of snitching. Whatever you have to do, do it. You will be protected by me. Also, I want y'all to move some heavy dope. I've noticed that heroin is booming in this state. There are too many requests for it; so, I have decided to amp up the quantity. As of next week, I will be flooding the streets with potent dope and pills. All I need you and Totta to do is move twenty-two bricks of heroin. Can you fellas handle those tasks?"

"Hell yes," I replied before Dank could nod his head.

That was enough money for us to go legit, if we wanted to.

"Very well then."

"I'm hearing there is some static in Baymatch's old territories. Who are you going to appoint it to?" Ruger asked out of nowhere.

"As of right now, no one. None of those niggas are doing right. I'm heavily thinking about shutting the drugs off that street. They need to learn some fucking manners. I will not have my empire crumble because they have any and everyone selling dope. Matter of fact, my crew minus Dank and Totta, I want y'all to cease the drugs being supplied to them. Make sure that if any of those niggas try to step somewhere else that they be apprehended instantly and brought to me," she voiced in a creepy voice.

"Yes, Chief," they stated in unison as they hopped to their feet with cell phones in their hands.

"So, it will be a drought on the Westside, basically?" I inquired, giving her my full attention.

"Actually, it will be a drought in the entire city. I gotta let them know that I mean fucking business. I'm tired of killing those snitching fuckers. Every time I turn around, I'm cutting niggas up or having them placed in prison for the rest of their lives. Take away their need to eat, and they will get in compliance. I did my uncle's crew like that for a month, and that got those fuckers on board...real fast."

"How long will the drought last?" Dank probed.

"Until I have the mass shipment of heroin. I just put the order in today and not on a rush order at that. You guys are saved from the drought since I will be paying y'all for your services. Once my needs are fulfilled, then you guys will be out of my protection and back to the two-man team that y'all are, unless y'all want to become more affiliated with The Savage Clique," she voiced while looking at each of us.

Clearing his throat, Dank spoke, "I'm thinking about getting out the game and going legit. I got a little one on the way and a wonderful chick on my team."

Nodding my head, I said, "I'm getting out as well after we do this for you. I'm in the same boat as Dank. It's time to be a family man and live an honest life."

X's eyes shown me something that I never saw her show, love and compassion.

"I admire you guys more than y'all think I do. I'm thinking about leaving it behind as well. As you know I been in the streets since I was fourteen. I built an unbreakable empire. I want the same things y'all do. Love is such a beautiful thing. It's a feeling that I can't describe; yet, I'm yearning to get it and hold onto it."

"Then leave it behind, X," I said.

"I will, but I have an important matter that I must clean up first. Then, I will be able to sit back and be a family woman. It's something that I wanted for a long time."

"If you don't remember nothing else that I tell you, X, please remember this...nothing or no one can stop you but you," Dank voiced passionately.

When that nigga said that, I felt it in my spirit, causing me to look at him and nod my head.

Chapter 13
Jonzella

Sunday, March 5ᵗʰ

Ever since the wee hours on Saturday morning, Totta was different. He sexed, held, and cared for me differently. It was as if someone had spoken something into him, turning him into a different type of loving being. I didn't question what had taken over him. I just let him be as he was becoming into the man that I knew he was capable of being.

"Are you hungry, Queen?" Totta inquired as my cell phone rang.

"No," I replied as I placed my device in my hand.

Kyvin's name displayed across the screen, and I sighed heavily.

"Who is that you don't want to answer for?"

"My brother, Kyvin."

"Oh," he replied as he snuggled closer to me.

With a smile on my face, I loved our intimacy. It was even better than before him leaving the house Friday evening.

As I swiped my thumb across the answer option, I said hello before I placed the phone to my ear.

"Hey, Jonzella. What are you up to?" Kyvin inquired.

"Lying down. What's up?" I replied in a nonchalant timbre.

"I wanted to know whether you have talked to Mom and Dad."

"I talked to Dad some days ago. Why? What's up?" I asked, sitting upright in the bed.

"Just wanted to know whether he was talking strangely? Was Mom sounding different?"

"When I talked to Dad, he was his normal self," I lied.

"I think he is involved in some heavy shit, Jonzella. I don't know what it is, but I am determined to find out."

"What makes you think he's involved in anything?"

"Let's just say that he's been up here visiting one of the ladies that he's been cheating on Mom with. Also, I've seen him with a group of men that I know he shouldn't be around. The same type of guys he warned Jonsey about. He's dealing with guys of that nature here in the city I live in."

"Are you sure?" I inquired, trying to sound curious.

"Yes, I am. I need you and Jonsey to be safe when y'all are around him."

In need of telling him to back off, I couldn't get the words out of my mouth. The last thing I wanted was for Kyvin to go up against the one man that had two of his three sons killed. Dad would have no problem getting rid of Kyvin's ass anyway, just because of his sexual preference.

"Well, I gotta get back to work. I will call you later. Okay?" he stated in a sincere voice.

"Okay."

Ending the call, I placed my cell phone on the end table before exiting the bed.

"Where are you going?"

"To chat with Jonsey for a second," I told Totta as I turned around to look at him.

"You might want to call her. She left with Dank earlier this morning. They are staying at his crib for a couple of days."

Nodding my head, I sauntered my behind back to the bed. Sighing heavily as I lie underneath my man, I thought on Kyvin's and me conversation. I was so far in the zone that it took Totta to shake me several times before I was brought to reality.

"What got your mind boggled?" he voiced as he placed light kisses on my arm.

"The conversation that I had with Kyvin."

"What about it?"

"He just told me that he thinks our Dad is involved in some kind of illegal activities with the same type of guys he's warned Jonsey about. He called to inform us to be safe around him and our mother."

"Then, I suggest you listen to your brother. You know I'm locked and loaded at all times. I don't mind putting--," he stated before I cut him off.

"We are not even going there, Totta. Our father will not harm us."

"How can you be so sure?"

"Because we have to act like we don't know what he's done or who he really is, which is a certified fucking OG of whatever it is that he does."

"No disrespect or anything, if that nigga come to you wrong you...I'm going to handle him the only way I know how," Totta stated, seriously.

"I know but trust me when I say that my father isn't any harm to me...I meant that. Now, let's get off that subject. I wanna talk about you and what has gotten into you," she announced while lying in the crook of my arms.

With a smile on his face, he asked, "What are you talking about, guh?"

"You know exactly what I'm talking about," I hissed in a sexy manner.

"On some real shit, it's time for a brother to settle down, and I wanna settle down with you. We already got a little one on the way. I don' already attempted to kill a broad not only because she was running her mouth, but because she was going to be an issue for you and our child. I wasn't having any of that shit. I had a talk with the most powerful Queenpin this nation has ever seen. She said some real shit to me and Dank, and I had to admit that she was dead ass right. So, I'm going to love you way better than I did before. I want you and no one else. I can honestly say that I cannot live without you, Jonzella. I refuse to live without you."

Tears welled in the corner of my eyes as I held the biggest smile. The joy I felt was phenomenal; if I was going to have this very feeling for the rest of my life, then I was one lucky woman.

"Remember when I told you that I was entertaining the thought of leaving the streets if you wanted me to?" he inquired while rubbing the side of face.

"Yeah. You must've changed your mind or something?" I asked, giving him my full attention.

"No I haven't, but I gotta complete something before I'm able to leave the streets behind. What I have to do will require for me and Dank to be out in the streets more than what we have been lately. The reason I'm telling you this is because I don't want any secrets between us. I want you to know what is going on with me at all times."

"Okay. Thank you for letting me into that thick head of yours," I stated seriously before continuing, "How long will you be doing your thing?"

"Until all the dope is distributed and we teach the little runts what happens when you snitch," he voiced calmly as he continued stroking my face.

"All that I ask of you is that you and Dank make it back to us. Make sure that y'all don't get caught up in nobody's shit," I informed him as I placed the tip of my nose on his oily nose.

Breathing heavily, Totta glared in my eyes before saying, "I love you, and I meant that."

"I know, and you best to believe that I love you as well," I stated before we engaged in a passionate kiss.

That sloppy, passionate kiss turned into us sucking on each other's bottom lip. Our hands traveled over each other bodies. Before I knew it, we were in the sixty-nine position. My mind was blown at the things Totta was doing to me. My eyes seemed as if they were never going to stop rolling in the back of my head while I was slobbing him down. With a mouthful of dick, I gently kneaded his balls.

"Shittt," he groaned while attacking my pussy with his wonderfully long, wet tongue.

Our foreplay was a long, delicate yet passionate one. One that I would've never thought would occur between us. I must say that I didn't have any complaints. I wasn't into swallowing sperm, but Totta deserved for me to give him the ultimate mind blower.

Honestly, I thought he would've gotten tired of licking and sucking on me; shoot, I was dead wrong. My man made me cum several times before I had the chance to drain his dick dry.

"I need this pussy now, Jonzella," he groaned, tapping me on my ass.

"You'll get it when I'm ready for you to have it," I whined after I stopped sucking on the head of his dick.

Growling, Totta replied, "Jonzella, I need to be inside of you now."

With a frown on my face, I pulled my mouth off his dick. Turning around to straddle him, Totta had a look on his face that made me want to fuck him all night long. Taking the head of his dick and rubbing it against my clit, I moaned loudly.

"Put him in you!" he shouted while gripping my thighs.

The moment I inserted him inside of me, my juices rushed out of me. I didn't do well with being yelled at. Every time Totta decided that he wanted to raise his voice at me, I made it my motherfucking business to take it out on him. I rode him until he begged for me to stop.

"Why should I stop?" I inquired seductively as I slowed my motions, followed by rocking back and forth on the dick.

"Mane, you ain't finna have me in here hollering like a broad. Nawl, I ain't going out like that," he hissed in a sexy way.

The noise he made turned me on, and I couldn't help but go dumb on the dick.

Not able to take what I was rendering to his body, Totta flipped me over as if I was a pancake and wore my pussy out. He started punishing me like I disobeyed him.

As he pounded in my pussy, he calmly spoke, "You ever think about leaving me, I'mma make sure yo' ass in a casket."

Oh wow, I thought while pulling the bed sheets of the mattress.

"Do you fucking hear me, Jonzella?" he barked, slamming his dick further inside of me, hitting the spot that caused my body to go limp.

I couldn't respond; thus, he repeated the question again.

"Yes. I hear you, Dadddyy!"

"If I catch a nigga in your face, I'mma murk his ass and hold you hostage in the house. Do you understand me?" he questioned as he maneuvered his dick to the left corner of my pussy, which instantly caused my body to start shaking as I yelped out his name.

An hour later, Totta and I were lying naked in the bed, out of breath and glaring at each other. I felt sleep coming heavily upon me. I didn't want to move as his sperm seeped out of me.

"Come on and let's take a shower," he voiced before placing a kiss on my lips.

"Not right now, baby, I'm sleepy."

Chuckling, he said, "So, you finna knock out this early?"

"Trust, I'll wake back up and be ready for another round."

"You need to eat. You really haven't ate nothing today," he voiced as he rubbed my belly.

"I don't feel like cooking."

"You act like I don't know how to cook. What do you want to eat?"

"Whatever you having," I replied, closing my eyes.

"A'ight," he stated before leaving the bed.

I didn't know when he left the bedroom. My eyes were shut just that quick. I was awakened by the smell of a wonderful meal and Totta loudly stating that it was time for me to get up.

Doing as he instructed, I sat upright while rubbing my eyes.

"How long have I been sleep?"

"An hour," he replied while placing a plate on the end table.

"Food looks delicious, baby."

"Daddy got skills guh...better act like you know it."

After I placed my plate on top of the pillow, Totta exited the room. Before I dug into the fried pork chops, buttery, cheesy rice, and corn on the cob, I prayed over my food. Once I was done, Totta was walking in the room with his plate and a cup of orange juice.

Handing me the cup, he voiced, "Don't forget to take your prenatal vitamins."

With a smile on my face, I said, "I won't."

As we ate, we barely talked. I was exhausted; whereas, I believed Totta was thinking about him and Casey's situation. All I knew was that their asses better make it back in one piece, with no criminal charges attached to their names.

After I finished eating, I showered. Still sleepy, I knew I couldn't go because my pink bud was awakened the moment Totta spoke.

"Come sit on my face, I need dessert before I hit the streets."

Damn near running to him, I was eager to get to the one man that made my body and mind weak. A sister was starting to get used to having his face planted in between my legs. With cocked eyes, a dry mouth, and a twerking body, I fed my man his dessert with pride. Halfway done with feeding my man his dessert, there were several hard knocks on the door.

"Who in the fuck is knocking on your door like that?" Totta questioned angrily as we stopped having sex.

"I don't know, but they ain't finna stop what we got going on," I voiced as I tried to continue what we had going on.

However, Totta wasn't on the same page as me. He told me to get up. Without hesitation but a lot of huffing and puffing, I was off him. As he put his clothing on, the knocks continued. Placing his pistol in his hand, Totta exited my room.

Halfway down the hallway, he sternly voiced, "Who is it?"

I didn't hear who was at the door. However, the moment Totta opened the door, I heard the one person that I thought I would never hear or see again.

"Is Jonsey Brown here?" Demante Wilks asked.

"Oh shit, I gotta tell Jonsey she needs to stay with Dank for some days until Demante get his ass away from this city," I voiced as I scrambled towards the other side of my bed.

As I dialed her number, Totta said, "Nawl, don't nobody by the name of Jonsey Brown live here."

"A'ight," Demante stated before the door closed at the same time Jonsey answered her phone.

"Hello," she cooed in the phone. I knew what she had going on; thus, I was going to make the call simple and short.

"Don't come back to the house no time soon. Demante Wilks just showed up for you. Don't worry, Totta told him that no one lives here by your name."

After telling Casey to stop doing whatever it was that he was doing, Jonsey stated, "Oh shit. We have to move, ASAP. I'm going to curse Dad out something awful. He is the reason why that bastard knows where we live."

"I highly doubt that. It could've been those crazy ass brothers of ours, God rest their souls," I announced as Totta stood in the doorway.

"What did he say? Was he angry?" she questioned.

In the background, Casey said, "Why in the fuck is you worried about another nigga, Jonsey? Mane, you better get yo' damn mind right. For those dumb ass questions, I gotta punish you now."

Trying my best to push out the naughty images of them fucking, I quickly said, "He wanted to know did you live here...that's it, and he didn't sound angry."

By the time I finished my sentence, I heard smacking and spanking noises in the background. Jonsey didn't respond but I heard soft mumbling as if she was groaning in the pillow. If Casey was anything like Totta, I knew Jonsey wasn't going to be able to hang up the phone; therefore, I ended the call.

"I'm only going to ask this question once and once only...is that dude an issue?"

"Not for me, but for Jonsey, hell yes."

CHAPTER 14
Casey

I wore Jonsey's ass out. She was doing the most for me, wanting to know what the next nigga had to say. Damn right, I was feeling salty behind that shit. That was, until she told me the story behind the ex-nigga. I felt a little bad for how I beat her hot, juicy pussy up; on the other hand, I was very sure that she enjoyed being dicked.

"Aye, what's up with school?" I asked as she sauntered from the bathroom, wearing one of my black T-shirts.

"I haven't been in minute. I went on a little sick leave. I'll be back in there Tuesday."

"And work?"

"I'll be back there Tuesday as well," she replied, taking a seat on the edge of the bed.

"Are you ready to get back to your normal life?"

"Yes. It's boring being at home all day. Plus, I got a full scholarship to ASU, so I need to take advantage of that free money."

"When will you walk across the stage?" I asked as I massaged her back.

"I don't know now. With a baby on the way, I know I will have to sit out the fall semester. Then, I probably won't be able to take a full load in the spring of next year. I have to chat with my academic advisors when I return to school."

"You do know I'm going to be involved in you and our child's lives, right? I'm not going to be a weekend man or dad. I'm going to be full-time man and dad. If you want to sit out for the fall or not, I'm behind you one-hundred percent."

She nodded her head and sighed. Jonsey had been in a funk majority of the day, except for when we were having sex. I was determined to know what had her mind boggled. Placing her in my lap, I asked her what was wrong. She told me nothing. Not the one to give up, I made Jonsey tell me what was on her mind.

Looking into my eyes, she bit down on her bottom lip before saying, "I'm scared of being a mother. It sort of terrifies me. What if I get it wrong? What if I'm not good enough, you know? What if I can't juggle school, work, myself, you, and our baby? How will all this work out and I not lose my mind?"

Chuckling while rubbing her face, I replied, "You are going to be a great mom. There is no need to be terrified. We are going to learn everything that we need as far as the simple stuff like baby proofing this house, what to expect when you go into labor, and the first six weeks after you give birth, and all that other shit. As far as school, work, personal time, me and our child, I'm going to be there to help you along the way. Everything will be fine. Plus, our baby has two grandmothers that will spoil the hell out of him or her. We will be okay, Jonsey, so don't worry about that."

"Okay," she stated lowly before biting on her bottom lip.

"You did catch the part where I said we will baby proof *this* house, right?" I inquired seriously.

There was no need in her finding an apartment when I had an entire house big enough for the three of us.

"Yes, I caught it," she stated with a smile on her face.

The smile told me what she thought, yet I had to know what she was really thinking; thus, I asked, "What do you think about you moving in with me?"

"Umm," she stated before continuing, "As long as you aren't a control freak and want to have things your way, then I'm okay with it."

With a huge grin on my face, I excitedly said, "That's what's up. So, when are you planning on moving in?"

"I'm not sure yet. More than likely when school is over for the summer. That would be the perfect time to move."

"Cool. We can redecorate the crib if you would like."

"I will take that into consideration," she voiced sweetly as she rubbed the lower part of my right arm.

Time passed before either of us said a thing. The doorbell rang, bringing our personal time to a halt.

"Let me go see who's at the door," I informed her as she rolled off my legs.

As I skated down the stairs, my doorbell started doing numbers, and the only person that I know will play on my doorbell like that was that fool, Totta.

"Stop playing on my shit, Totta!" I yelled.

"Well, hurry your ancient black ass up and open this damn door," he laughed followed by a female voice chuckling, which I recognized as Jonzella's voice.

As soon as I opened the door, Totta was with the shits. He came in the house, joking.

Shaking my head, I said, "What do you want?"

"Well, my brother from another mother...you will have a problem from a nigga name Demante Wilks. If he is your problem, then he becomes my problem. All four of us need to talk about this character, followed by you and me hitting the streets for a little while...to do our duties."

Before I could open my mouth to respond, Jonsey was upstairs going the fuck off.

"Who in the fuck gave you the right to give anyone my damn address? What kind of father does that shit?" she yelped in the phone, which caused Jonzella to ask me quickly whether she could go upstairs.

Nodding my head, I waltzed towards the front room and took a seat. Totta plopped his ass in his favorite recliner. We remained silent as we listened to Jonsey telling her father a thing or two while Jonzella tried to calm her down.

"I don't give two fucks about none of that shit you are talking about. You are foul, dude. I wouldn't give a damn if you would never speak to me, again," she spat before the room grew quiet.

Shortly afterwards, the sisters began arguing, which led me to believe that the conversation between their father and Jonsey had ended.

"You gotta be careful how you talk to him, Jonsey. He is into some shit. I talked to Kyvin today, and he said that Dad is tied into some thuggish niggas. So, keep that man at a distance but not too much of a distance where you are placed on his radar," Jonzella stated, calmly.

"You acting like you scared of the nigga or something. I wish he would try that shit on me that he did to Kevin and Kenny," Jonsey spat.

As they went back and forth, Totta and I touched on the topic of the ladies' father.

"Shid, it seems like we might have to knock that nigga off."

"Yep," I replied with a serious look upon my face.

"What we gonna do about that nigga Demante?" Totta asked.

The mentioning of the cat's name prompted me to call Jonsey downstairs at the same time Totta called Jonzella. They sauntered down the stairs with different facial expressions. Jonesy was upset; whereas, Jonzella seemed worried. They took a seat, inches away from each other. While Jonzella sighed, I told them to give Totta and me the rundown on the dude Jonsey used to date, and how their father was tied into the nigga.

After they told us what happened, I knew then that Jonsey was moving out first thing in the morning. I spoke my mind on her leaving their duplex at once. She wasn't hearing what I had to say, and I turned deaf upon her trying to reason with me. There was no way in hell she was going to be in an environment where she wasn't safe if Totta and I weren't there.

"Tomorrow, I'm going to get a pistol license, and I would love it if you purchase me a gun. I'm not ready to move out yet. I don't want to rush moving in with you. Like I stated earlier, I want to finish out this semester then we can move my things over here," she voiced sternly.

Sighing heavily, I said, "Okay, Jonsey. In the morning, we will take care of the license and gun, and we'll going to the gun range."

"Do y'all have any idea what y'all father really could be into?" Totta inquired.

They shook their heads.

"Do y'all feel that he may become a threat, eventually?"

Clearly, there was mixed emotions as Jonzella shook her head as Jonsey nodded hers.

"Well, Jonzella you already know where I stand if he crosses you," Totta voiced while looking at her.

"I know there shouldn't be a reason I need to state the same thing to you Jonsey. So, this is what I suggest…either you keep that nigga at a distance like Jonzella said or cut his ass off completely."

"Okay," she replied softly as my stomach growled.

"Now, back to this Demante dude. Why in the fuck would he be down here?" I asked, looking at the ladies.

"I assume to get me back or he could be on some revenge shit. Who knows," Jonsey stated, hopping away from the sofa.

"One damn thing I do know if he keeps on coming around I'mma blast his ass," Jonzella stated boldly.

Ring. Ring. Ring.

Jonzella's phone rang. Looking at the screen, she sighed heavily before rejecting the call.

"Who was that?" Totta inquired in unison.

"Renee."

"Oh," he replied at the same time. Jonzella's phone rang again. This time she answered.

"Hello," she stated in a cool timbre.

The way she spoke in the phone had my partner on alert mode. He sat upright in the recliner as he looked at his woman talking on the phone.

"Yes, I'm fine Dad. Why do you ask that?"

In a matter of second, she quickly stated, "He just came to the house looking for Jonsey."

"I don't know what kind of car he was in," she replied in the phone.

After she said that statement, it seemed as if the color in her face was drained.

Jonsey, Totta, and myself asked in a low timbre, "What is he saying to you?"

As she placed the call on speakerphone, Totta waltzed towards her and took a seat.

"I want you and Jonsey to get to a safe place until I arrive down there. Those dumb ass brothers of y'all's led them fools straight to y'all. Demante has been seeking Jonsey for quite some time. I refused to tell him where she was. I may have done a lot of bad things but placing y'all in harm's way is not what I ever had in mind. She's so angry with me, and I'm not understanding why. Can you please talk some sense into her, Jonzella?"

On the verge of opening her mouth, Jonsey decided not to say anything the moment Jonzella looked at her. Instantly, Jonzella came to Jonsey's defense.

"Dad, you set her up to be with Demante in the first place, and then, you had the nerves to punish her for falling in love with one of your workers. You intentionally placed her in harm's way when you decided to place them together. How am I to talk sense into someone that already has sense? It seems that you are the one needing some sense talked into you. I don't care what you do in your spare or full-time. All I ask is that you stop trying to come for Jonsey."

"Who in the fuck are you talking to in that manner, Jonzella?" their father questioned nastily.

"You, Dad," she replied in the same tone as he did.

"I am going to call you tomorrow, and you better have your damn mind right. The same way I got these street niggas in compliance, my fucking children will be in compliance as well."

"See that's where you got the game fucked up at...we ain't your fucking soldiers, Dad. We are your children. You can't put them and us in the same category," Jonsey spat before Jonzella could respond.

"I'm not about to argue with either of you. I will be in Alabama within the next twenty-four hours. I suggest y'all get to a safe place like I said," their father replied before ending the call.

"Turn them cell phones off," I told them.

On command, they did what I demanded of them.

"Dank and I got some business to handle. Neither of y'all leave this house. We will be gone for at least four hours. I'm very sure he won't mind y'all eating up his groceries," Totta voiced as he handed Jonzella his .380.

After we kissed the ladies, we headed out the door. As soon as we sat in Totta's whip, he fired up a blunt.

As he reversed out of my yard, my mind was on full throttle. I had to see what the fuck was up with their father. I had a bad vibe about that nigga, and I sure as hell didn't want him around my child or my lady. That motherfucker had to go; he was doing too much for me.

Halfway to our destination, Totta said, "You good, mane?"

"Yeah, I'm good."

"Do you think these little runts will listen to what we have to say?"

"They will have no choice but to or they will be as good as dead by the end of the week. X ain't playing with their asses."

"Truth be told, I think the only way they are going to know she means business is by showing her face and sending out her signal."

"True. Well, we will discuss that when we have a meeting Wednesday night. Maybe her coming out will put those motherfuckas in their places."

"That too, but you know how she gets when she see some fuck shit...she brings out those damn machetes. It would be a fucking bloodbath by the time she's done fucking up the city," I voiced as I inhaled what was left of the blunt.

Totta was talking as my phone rang. Looking at my device, I saw Danzo's name.

When I answered my phone, Totta stopped talking.

"Yo," I spat.

"Aye mane, what in the fuck is going on in the city?" he asked curiously as he inhaled.

With a puzzled look on my face, I asked, "What you talking about?"

"Mane, several people tried to put in order for some work, and they are told that ain't shit being shipped out right now. I mean these niggas called locally, then they called some folks in Georgia, Florida, Mississippi, Tennessee, California, Seattle, South Carolina, Michigan, and New York. Ain't nobody doing shit, what in the fuck is going on?"

"What is you talking about?" I asked, playing dumb.

The way he came on the phone had me questioning whether this nigga was an informant. He had never discussed any important business like that over the phone.

"Mane, it seems like it's finna be a massive drought flowing through this bitch. But why, though? Who pissed X off?" Danzo inquired.

Totta swerved off the road because he was looking at me with a shocked facial expression. Danzo was on some bold shit; never have we ever called out the Queenpin's name over the damn phone or in certain people's cars. I knew then it was time for me to get off the phone with Danzo. He was on some fuck shit, and I wasn't with it.

Chuckling, I replied, "Aye, mane, I'm chilling with my lady. I gotta go."

Not willing to let me off the phone, Danzo continued, "So, what in the hell are we supposed to do?"

"Mane, didn't I just tell you I was chilling with my lady?" I stated, angrily.

"Yeah," he replied in a tone that I didn't like.

"Notify X of that fuck shit, my nigga. Danzo know too much shit. He gotta go. There are some cops out there that are legit and ain't with the shit that we be doing," Totta voiced as soon as I ended the call with Danzo.

"I'm already on it," I said as I dialed J-Money's number.

As the phone rang, Totta said, "That nigga Danzo gotta go; he showing signs of an informant."

Before I could respond to my partner, J-Money answered the phone, "Yo'."

"Where you at, woe?"

"Shid, chillin' at Legion's crib," he replied while inhaling.

"We finna pull up then."

"Bet," he replied before we ended the call.

As I stuffed my cell phone in the holster, Totta said, "Legion's crib."

"You know it."

"Well, I guess it's really finna be a happy hunting night for The Savage Clique."

Chapter 15
Jonsey

I didn't miss being at my job at all; however, I was glad that I wasn't at home or at Casey's place. He was starting to smother the shit out of me. Every time I turned around he was asking me questions about how I was feeling, or what I was thinking about if I was quiet for too long. That shit was driving me crazy.

Work was work. It didn't take customers or my co-workers long to agitate the hell out of me. It seemed like as soon as I was off to myself, enjoying the peace and quiet while performing my job duties, one of those fuckers would interrupt.

My lunch break was pure hell and then some. Fredericka's ass wanted to chat about the things that took place while I was gone. He went so far as to tell me what ass he played in the past couple of weeks. When I learned who Fredericka was talking about, I spit my soda all over myself. I had to excuse myself from the conversation that he was happily telling me about.

I was glad when my time arrived for me to haul ass. I fled Wal-Mart so fast that one could've thought that someone was chasing me.

Now sitting in my math class, I was ready to go to Casey's home. My mind wasn't on school; it was on Demante and what he wanted with me. I couldn't think straight knowing that he was in the same city as I was. I didn't have a clue as to what could possibly be on his mind.

Zit. Zit. Zit.

I felt the strong vibrations from my cell phone in my pocket. Pulling it out, I saw that my father was calling. Sighing heavily, I ignored the call. Afterwards, I shoved my phone into my book bag. My next two courses took forever to end. When it did, I flew to my car. Jonzella was yelling my name as I approached the first parking lot.

Turning around quickly, I sighed heavily.

As she took her precious time coming to me, I cleared my throat, followed by saying, "You can speed the fuck up, you know."

When she was close to me, Jonzella glared at me before saying, "What's up with the attitude?"

"I'm agitated as hell. This day has dragged on long enough. I just want to go to the crib, get some clothes, and go over to Casey's place," I stated as we began to walk towards the second parking lot.

"Our parents are here. They been here. They are staying at Embassy Suites."

"Why are you telling me?" I asked while rolling my eyes. I didn't give a damn where their sneaky asses were staying.

"Because they want to have dinner with us and the men that we are dating tonight. It's not a request, bitch, it's a demand; thus, you need to get your shit together and be cordial, Jonsey."

"I don't think I have anything to say to them. How in the hell can you be in their presence?" I asked, coming to a complete stop and looking at her.

"They are who they are. They are no different than the niggas we are pregnant by. Who said Mom had anything to do with Kevin and Kenny not living? Dad sure as hell didn't say she had a hand in it."

"I'm not coming to that damn dinner date y'all set up. I'll take a rain check on that shit."

As we made it to our cars, Jonzella went on and on about why I should be present at the family dinner date.

The moment I unlocked my door, I hopped in. Jonzella was still running her damn mouth. I was not in the mood to hear a lecture from her. I just wanted to be left alone.

Placing my key in the ignition, I said, "You have a pleasant time with our parents. You can tell them whatever you want. I refuse to entertain their asses."

Pulling off on my sister, I left the campus. As I drove towards the home Jonzella and I shared, I thought about the severe time I had with Demante. Father wasn't hearing any of the things that I had to say about loving that dude. He wanted to know why I was so weak for a nigga that couldn't do anything for himself, let alone be able to provide for me. As I thought about all the unnecessary shit I went through because of my love for Demante, I couldn't figure out why my daddy did what he did to me.

"Fuck that. I'm going to that damn dinner date to ask his ass some questions," I stated aloud as I reached in the passenger seat, aiming for my book bag.

Retrieving my phone out of the front of book bag, I dialed Jonzella's number. On the third ring, she answered the phone.

"Hello," she stated casually.

"Where is this dinner date taking place?" I inquired as I drove down Highland Avenue.

"We will decide when they come over. So, you decided to go?"

"Yep. I got some questions for Father's stank ass," I stated while slowing down my vehicle, thanks to seeing a police car parked on the curb.

"I hope you behave."

"I sure will," I replied, sarcastically.

"I'm serious, Jonsey. I don't want you to have a major blow up," she fussed as if she was the mother.

Not in the mood for her, I sighed heavily before saying, "You know it's not safe to drive and be on the phone. I will talk to you once you get home."

"Okay," she replied with an attitude.

Ending the call, I threw my phone on the passenger seat.

As I drove down the heavily populated street, I analyzed the community. It had so much potential to be more than what it was. There were quite a few homes that were decent, as the others weren't. The people that frequented or lived in the homes were your average hood people. Loud, obnoxious, and ignorant at all costs; they acted as if they didn't have the good sense that God blessed them with.

After I made a right turn on Ann Street, I was thankful that I was close to my home, I sighed heavily as I rapidly pulled into the driveway. Turning off the engine, I hopped out of my car. Ambling towards the door, I saw my father's car strolling up the dead-end road.

"Ugh, I don't want to be dealing with this man at this particular time and moment," I voiced, strolling towards my front door.

As I opened the door of my home, my father's voice was loud and clear as he spoke to me. I gave him a dry wave before ambling into the house. Halfway to my room, I heard Jonzella's happy voice conversing with our father.

Damn, how fast was she going? I left her ass in the parking lot, I thought while rolling my eyes and exhaling sharply.

"Jonsey!" my father stated as he walked inside of our home.

"Yeah," I replied as I continued packing my clothes.

"Don't you answer me like that, young lady?" he voiced sternly as he strolled down the hallway.

"You're in my house, Father."

"I don't care about none of that shit you are talking about, Jonsey. At the end of the damn day, I am the father...not you," he voiced while standing in the threshold of my door.

I ignored him as he continued running his motherfucking mouth. Once I finished packing my clothes and shoes, I waltzed passed him as if he wasn't standing inches away from me.

"Oh, you smelling yourself again, huh?" he voiced nastily before aggressively grabbing my left wrist and turning me around to face him.

"Don't you ever touch me like that again. You must got me mistaken with those little whores you are fucking!" I spat while rolling my eyes.

Before I knew it, my father slammed me against the wall while glaring into my eyes.

"Father, please be calm," Jonzella voiced in a scared timbre as she ran towards us.

"Jonzella, stay out of this, darling. This has been long overdue. Jonsey's running around acting like I owe her something when in fact I don't owe her a motherfucking thing," he replied in a calm tone while glaring into my eyes.

Continuing, our father said, "You better learn to stay in a child's place. I am not the one to piss off, and I'm sure you know that. I do what the fuck I want to do. You do what you can. There is a difference between you and me, and you better learn who in the fuck you are dealing with."

Understanding exactly what he was saying, I shook my head as tears streamed down my face.

"Do you understand what I'm saying to you, Jonsey Brown?" he questioned, sternly.

"You better get your motherfucking killer hands off me, or it will be some damn issues in Alabama," I told him as if he was a regular guy in the streets.

Chuckling, he removed his hands away from me as he backed away.

As I walked away, my father stated clearly, "You need to tread lightly when dealing with me, little girl."

His statement pushed me over the edge, causing me to quickly turn around and waltzed towards him. Jonzella tried her best to calm me down while placing her cool hands on my arms, all the while begging me to let things go.

Ignoring my sister, I yelped, "No, motherfucker, you need to tread lightly around me! I should be the bitch you are scared of. I don't give a fuck that you are a weak ass, pussy ass killer of your own children. Also, I don't give a fuck that you are OG of some sorts. None of that matters to me. So, the best thing you can do is stay the fuck away from me! When I learned that you had Kenny and Kevin killed, you became nothing to me. Just how Jonzella feels for Renee, I feel the same way about you and Mom."

The squabble continued until there were three strong knocks on the open door as a strong voice male said, "Is Jonzella Brown here?"

"Yes, I am," she replied in a calm tone as her body went rigid.

Turning around to see why my sister's body went still, mine did as well.

"May I talk with you for a moment, ma'am?" the tall, handsome White officer asked as his short, sun burned, not so cute partner looked throughout our home from the threshold of the door.

"Sure," she replied as she released my arms.

"And what do you have to speak with my daughter about?" our father inquired as he began walking towards the living room.

I wasn't about to leave because I didn't know what they were going to discuss with my sister; thus, I took a seat while giving them my full attention. I prayed that they weren't there about the gun that killed Zabriah's crazy ass. I was on pins and needles as I didn't want Jonzella caught up in my shit.

"Ms. Brown, do you own a chrome .22?" the tall, handsome officer asked.

"Yes, I do. May I ask why you are inquiring about my gun?" she asked.

Clearing his throat, he said, "Because your gun was used in a homicide."

Jonzella was taken aback as my father shouted, "What in the hell?"

Playing the role that I knew she would play, Jonzella shook her head and said, "Now, that's impossible because I keep my gun in a safe place at all times. You must have me mistaken with someone else."

As they continued talking, it seemed as if my heart was going to burst out of my chest. I zoned out as they followed Jonzella down the hall.

When I tuned back into things, I heard her say, "Wow. Where is my gun? It was here two weeks ago."

I began fidgeting with my hands as I knew I had to say something. There was no way in hell Jonzella was going to get into trouble for something that I did.

On the verge of getting up, the officer asked, "Ms. Brown, you had no idea that your gun wasn't in the place that you put it?"

"No. I always put it in my top drawer and place clothing on top of it," she stated before doing her infamous fake cry.

"Is my daughter in any type of trouble?" my father inquired in a professional manner.

Ignoring my father, the officer asked, "Ms. Brown, did you know a Zabriah Matin?"

"No, sir," she replied honestly while sniffling.

"Once again, officers, is my daughter in any type of trouble?" our father stated in an agitated timbre.

"No, sir, she isn't. We had to inquire about the gun because it was registered to her."

"So, why are you still questioning her?" my father huffed.

"Because that's our job before this case is closed out."

Hearing his statement, I began to breathe a little easier.

"What do you mean 'before the case is closed out'?" my father inquired with a raised eyebrow.

"The night of the murder, there was a gentleman that confessed to killing the woman. The killer used your daughter's gun. When we asked him about the gun, he stated that it was the closest thing to him so he used it."

"Who was the killer that took my gun and murdered someone with it?" Jonzella inquired.

"We aren't able to answer that, ma'am."

"Yet, you have the nerves to come here and question her...the least you can do is tell us what motherfucker took my child's weapon to murder someone else with. Also, she has the right to know if she needs a lawyer for this crap."

"Calm down, sir. We are just doing our job. We had to come here as ordered. So, we are going to write this report as the gun was stolen, which she didn't know about until today," the officer inquired.

"Okay," my father and Joznella stated in unison.

Shortly afterwards, the four of them returned to the front room. The eerie silence drove me insane as I wanted to know why in the fuck they haven't left yet.

Looking into my father's face, I knew he had several questions running through his mind, and I sure as hell wanted to know the questions and the answers.

The officers cleared their throat before looking out of the door. The short one placed his eyes on me and glared at me for what seemed like forever before he smiled at me.

Instantly, I felt weird. The palms of my hands became sweaty as I tried to continue looking at him.

"You need to contact the city jail and ask them when your weapon will be released. Once they give you a date, you are free to pick it up," the tall officer stated with a pleasant smile on his face.

"Okay," Jonzella stated as she took a seat and rubbed her belly.

"Congratulations to the both of you," the short officer stated as he looked to Jonzella and me.

With a shocked facial expression, and a 'what the hell' comment from our father, the officers began to walk away. My father was stark still as he comprehended what the officer said to us.

As the tall officer walked to their patrol car, the short one turned around and said, "We are employees of your children's fathers' boss. You two are protected under their boss. You ladies have a nice day, and once again congratulations on being a mom."

As soon as the officers left our premise, Father ran to close the door.

Locking it behind him, he said, "What type of men are y'all dating?"

I leaned back on the sofa as Jonzella stretched out. Neither of us said a single word. It was none of his business who was blowing my back out!

"I asked y'all a motherfucking question and damn it I want the fucking answer!" he yelled.

After he finished yelling, I stood and grabbed my overnight bag.

"And where are you going, young lady?"

"To my man's house. Jonzella, if you need me...you know where I'll be at," I told her while eyeing our father down.

Sighing heavily, Father looked at me and made the ugliest face before speaking, "There is only one person that I know that has pull such as having police officers on their team, and I swear before God that you two better not be dealing with no niggas that's dealing with that type of female."

Laughing, I responded with, "Whoever she is, Father...I'm very sure she ain't that bad compared to you. Wouldn't you say so, Jonzella?"

Jonzella didn't respond as I strolled towards the front door.

Our father gently grabbed my right wrist and said, "Sweetie, I know that you hate me right now, but listen to me. You don't know the significance of the shit that you may be involved in based on who you are fucking. You don't know shit about the street life and what it can bring you. Honey, I've lived this life for so long that I can't escape it no matter what I try to do. It always finds its way back to me; thus, I do shit that I didn't want to do. Whoever y'all are dealing with, please cut those ties. If they disappoint their boss...she won't hesitate to kill them, you, and your babies. Hell, the babies won't even make it...for the simple fact that y'all will be dead."

Turning around to stare my father in the face, I saw that he was shaking in his boots. For the first time ever, I knew that my father was afraid someone.

With a huge smile on my face, I said, "Father, you are scared of the big bad wolf."

"And you should be, too. That woman has killed and had killed more people than cancer itself," he stated, causing me to laugh in his face before exiting my home.

CHAPTER 16
Totta

"If the nigga wanted to meet me, you should've let him. I don't have anything to hide, Jonzella," I fussed as she was in my kitchen preparing breakfast.

"But, I'm saying though, Totta...it doesn't make sense for you to meet the man. I want y'all to be far apart as possible," she stated as she sashayed her thick ass towards me.

"All I'm saying is I want to know what type of nigga y'all be dealing with when y'all leave to visit them at their crib, or when he pops up down here," I voiced while eyeing her sexy ass parade around the kitchen.

She didn't respond right away. My baby glared at me as if she had a question to ask me. Whatever she had to say, I knew that she was trying to figure out the best way to ask me.

Jonzella stared at me so long that I had to clear my throat and buck my eyes, to grab her attention. In a matter of seconds, she asked a question that I was not prepared to answer.

"I'm going to ask you one more time...who y'all employer is because she has my daddy shook."

I cleared my throat for the last time.

Sighing heavily, I said, "She's really not my employer. We owe her a favor, so she's like our temporary boss. She's a female no one wants to be on the other side of the fence with. That means they will be looking at death with no questions asked."

"How do y'all know this woman?" Jonzella asked while folding her arms.

"She gives us what we need, when we need it."

"Do you have her direct number?"

"No. We have some of the guys' phone numbers who's under her," I told her truthfully as I didn't take my eyes off her.

"Have you ever fucked her?"

"Hell no."

"Did you ever want to?" Jonzella inquired, curiously.

Clearing my throat, I swore I didn't want to answer that question, yet, I did.

Slowly, I nodded my head.

"Why didn't you?"

"I didn't want those problems," I replied quickly.

"What does that mean?"

"Let's just say, that *she's*...um...well, I rather keep it on the money tip and not the sex and money tip. It's not well to mix business and pleasure with a woman of that nature. She doesn't mind fucking you while in the process of snapping your fucking neck or sticking a knife through their chest as she's riding you. I didn't need that type of negativity in my life."

Chuckling, my lady said, "That lil' pussy deadly, huh?"

"You motherfucking right," I laughed while hopping up from the table.

Shaking her head, she glared at me before saying, "If she threw that pussy at you now, would you accept it?"

"Fuck no. I have everything I could ever need in you," I informed her while wrapping my arms around her waist.

"Is that so?" she asked while biting down on her bottom lip.

Nodding my head, I whined, "You know I hate when you bite that bottom lip of yours, right?"

"Yep. That's why I do it," she voiced seductively as she leaned her head closer to mine.

In a split second, I gently pushed her against the counter, dropping to my knees. Shoving her black boy shorts downwards, I blew on her pussy.

"My God," she cooed as she spread her legs.

Chuckling, I wasted no time planting my face in her hairless pussy. I needed that monkey juice something awful, and I wasn't going to be satisfied until she filled my mouth with her wonderful liquids.

"Ahhh!" she whimpered as her body shook uncontrollably.

Amping things up, I stuck two fingers inside of her while sucking on her clit. My dick reached its maximum thickness. As I ate my baby's soul away, I was anxious to slide inside of her. I never thought I would be falling for someone as hard as I did with Jonzella. I wanted to please her no matter where we were or who we were with. She always received my loving on sight, and I would forever give it to her on sight!

While howling from pleasure, my baby came in my mouth. I was pleased at the sight and feel of her body going limp. As her body was crumpling downwards, my body was rising. Strapping her shaky legs against my waist, Jonzella had tears sliding down her beautiful, glowing brown face. This wasn't the first time she had shed tears during our sexual activities; however, this time I believe I understood why her body allowed her to tear up during oral sex.

"I love you, Jonzella," I told her as I laid her across the clean kitchen table.

"Me love you more," she stated as her eyes leaked.

Sliding inside of her, Jonzella was eager to receive me as I was her. Slowly yet passionately thrusting inside of her, I wiped the falling tears as we made eye contact. The longer I looked into her eyes, the further I dug inside of her.

"Totttaa!" she cooed as she creamed on my dick.

"Yes, my lady?" I heard myself say as I continued looking at her.

Repetitive orgasms was what she received by the time I was ready to feed our child. The moment I picked up the pace from the slow deep strokes, Jonzella was throwing her pussy back bringing me to a place I never wanted to escape—pure pleasure.

Pulling her head closer to mine, I shoved my tongue in her mouth. The kiss didn't last long because my baby started crying. I thought I was hurting her, so I stopped.

"Why you stopped?" she sobbed as her body shook.

"I thought I was hurting you since you started crying," I told her as I held her face close to mine.

"No, don't stop. Keep going. It feels so good. My body feels different when you are inside of me...I don't know if it's because of the pregnancy or...or how you have been with me lately," she stated as she began moving that clenching pussy of hers.

Doing as my lady commanded, I didn't ask any more questions. With our matching thrusts, her cries and tight hugs, and my dire need to shower her with a wonderful, passionate love-making session, Jonzella's legs were stretched open as I plummeted the very spot I couldn't stay out of.

"Tottaaa, I'm cummin'!" she moaned as loud as she could.

My eyes were rolling in the back of my head as I said, "Me too."

Afterwards, we visited the shower. I thought she would've been tired or hungry after our shower. I was dead wrong; we went in for another round—in my bed. This time we didn't get a chance to finish since my doorbell and cell phone were ringing off the hook. Everybody and their mothers were calling me; yet, only one person made me stop making love to my woman—Dank.

Snatching the phone off the end table, I awkwardly said, "Yo'."

"I been ringing this damn doorbell for over thirty minutes. I know y'all asses ain't sleep, so open the door. Got some shit I need to holla at cha about," he voiced seriously.

"You do hear the way I'm talking, right?"

Chuckling, he replied, "I sure as hell do. Jonzella will be there for God knows how long. Open the door, mane."

"You got a fucking key, use it!" I stated loudly before huffing.

"Well, got damn it then, I will," he laughed as I ended the call.

"Business?" my lady asked with a pout on her face.

Sighing heavily as I kissed her on the forehead, I said, "I'm afraid so. I promise I will make this up to you."

"You better," she stated with a pleasant smile on her face.

As she got off me, I knew she was pissed, yet she didn't say a word. That was another reason why I loved that woman so much. She knew the life I was leading when she met me, and she was patient. She didn't pressure me to leave the streets behind, nor did she bitch when I had to leave out in the middle of the night. All she would say was 'make sure your black ass come back to me.'

After I took a quick shower, I ambled towards the kitchen. I knew that was where Dank's black ass would be at. I didn't make it far into the kitchen before hearing a utensil connect to a bowl or plate. As I entered my kitchen, I shook my head. I didn't utter a word as my homie sat at the table eating a bowl filled to the rim with Golden Grahams.

"I believe you are the one pregnant the way you be eating," I joked as I took a seat at the kitchen table.

"If I didn't know any better, I would think so, also," he replied quickly before continuing, "So, the word on the streets is that Danzo and two of them runts he be running with are missing."

"And?" I inquired as I kept my eyes glued on him.

"So, their folks raising all types of hell. The streets quiet, of course. I highly doubt anyone knows who snatched them niggas up since they left with bad bitches that are on X's team."

"And?" I stated, awaiting the real reason he was in my presence.

"That's it," he voiced while laughing.

With bucked eyes, I said, "Woe, I know you didn't come way over here, interrupted my sex session for a big bowl of damn cereal and some news that could've waited until later on today."

"J-Money and I had a bet on whether you would answer my call since Jonzella was over here," he laughed as a hard chuckle came from Dank's cell phone.

Growling, I said, "Mane, I know J-Money bet not be on that phone."

"I sure am, my nigga," his spat while laughing.

Growing angry, I said, "Mane, y'all on some hoe shit. Dank, get yo' ass out of my crib. I swear you play too fucking much mane."

Those fools busted into laughter. I was severely pissed at the games they played.

"Whatcha putting me out for?" Dank questioned as I pointed towards the front door.

"Mane, you don't want to know how much the bet was?" J-Money inquired while inhaling.

"Naw-," I quickly stated before recanting my answer. "Hell yes, I do want to know the amount because I want my damn cut," I told them.

The laughter roared from those fools' mouth before J-Money said, "The bet was... that you would stop fucking and answer the door and phone for him. All that was for a plate of food from the restaurant that serve that good ass soul food."

Laughing along with them niggas, I shook my head. I wanted to be mad, but I couldn't. Dank was always making stupid ass bets like that. His black ass always won a bet except for when I had my cousin step on his toes when he took Jonsey out on their first date. "Don't bring your black ass to my house no time soon. Next time you call you better make sure it's a real situation, or I'm gonna have Momma whoop your ass with that damn belt," I joked as I pushed my homie towards the front door.

Before he left my home, he ended the call with J-Money. Staring into my eyes, I knew he had some real shit to tell me. Thus, I placed my mind in professional mode.

"Did Jonzella tell you about the officers that came to the house and inquired about the gun?"

"Yeah," I replied, wondering where he was going with the topic.

"Did she tell what the officers said?"

"Yes."

"You don't find that odd that they knew exactly who we were fucking?"

Thinking heavily about what he was saying, I sighed heavily as I said, "You know X watches everyone. I guess it's all about collateral when it comes down to her."

Nodding his head, Dank responded with, "With that key information, we cannot fuck up this big dope drop she wants us to complete. You know she won't hesitate to do anything to them. This is my last drop. I should be set after that."

"This will be my last drop, also. I gotta think about the future of my little one and my lady. Do you know when X is going to flood the city with any work?"

"Nope. According to J-Money, he'll let us know when the next meeting will take place."

"Do you think he knows when the streets will be open for illegal activities?"

"You damn right that nigga knows," he stated honestly before placing his right hand on the doorknob.

As I nodded my head, we dapped each other up.

"Tell Jonsey I said what's up," I told him after he told me to tell Jonzella that he said hello.

"I will do. Aye, you wanna double date tonight?" he asked as he stepped onto the porch.

"Yeah. Hit me up with a time and place."

"A'ight," he stated as we dapped each other up for the final time. The moment I closed and locked the door, she purred my name— loud.

"This damn woman is going to wear my ass out," I voiced before smiling as I took my black ass to my bedroom.

CHAPTER 17
Jonzella

Monday, March 13th

I was thankful that the weekend had passed. I was tired of seeing my parents; they annoyed the hell out of Jonsey and me. Our mother didn't say much as she glared at us while being our father's cheerleader. His ass asked too many questions, which caused me to become annoyed. Then, he started with the demands of what he expected from us. Their last night in the city we had dinner together, and it didn't go smoothly.

In the beginning of the dinner, my poor sister barely said two words as she sat innocently at the round table. The look she gave our father let me know she was ready for war, and I was praying like hell she wouldn't start anything in those people's establishment. One thing about Jonsey when she was mad, the bitch was mad. She will say some shit that no one needs to hear.

Our father complained about not being able to meet Casey and Totta, and we didn't say anything as he complained. Neither of us wanted them to meet our father and for good reasons. Jonsey and our father argued from the time we began eating dessert until we left the restaurant. Then, he asked questions about the gun situation, the officers, and Demante.

I was clear cut about the gun situation and the officers; hell, the case was closed. As far as Demante, I didn't know if he came by our home or not since we were barely at home. I prayed like hell that he was gone for good. I didn't attempt to ask our father whether he ran into him. I wanted that part of the past to be gone forever more than Jonsey did. There were still unanswered questions as to why father sic'd Demante on Jonsey to begin with, followed by punishing her for being with him. Neither of us brought that up for closure.

Mother just stared as if she was scared to speak. I couldn't lie, our mother looked distraught. The woman that raised me didn't look the same at all. One minute, I could've sworn she was soulless. Her posture and the things that she would say had chills running through my body. I had to get away from her; she put me in the mind of a possessed individual. I didn't want that type of spirit on me. Thus, I pretended to be ill. Jonsey caught on to what I was doing. Not the one to be acting, Jonsey simply told them that it was time for her to go.

On the bright side of this past weekend, I truly enjoyed my time double dating with Casey and Jonsey. Our dating activities kicked off Friday night after Jonsey and I had dinner with our parents. We were grown ass individuals acting like little kids. Jonsey and I had full reign over what we did. We chose go-karting, gambling at the casino in Wetumpka, movies, and riding on the riverboat.

That damn Totta showed his ass on the boat. I knew it was going to be hard to ask him to take a five-day cruise into another land. The way he acted informed me that he was not with boats, life vests, and being on water. After he and Casey had several rounds of liquor, Totta was semi-okay. Of course, we ended the night on a lovely note—sexing until we couldn't anymore.

"Jonzella Brown," a petite, dark-skinned nurse stated after opening the door, interrupting my thoughts of the weekend.

With a smile on my face, I lifted from the chair as Totta did the same. As we strolled towards the nurse, I felt eyes on us. Turning my head to the right, I saw a couple of chicks staring at Totta. Loving their admiring eyes, I grabbed his hand. After he placed a kiss to the left side of my neck, one of the broads did a fake chuckle.

"How are you today?" the nurse asked the moment we were in her presence.

"Good, and you?" Totta and I responded in unison.

"Good. Thanks for asking," she announced bubbly as we followed behind her to the nurse's station.

Once she took my vitals and asked a series of questions, she led me into the examination room. Shortly after, she instructed me to dress in the paper gown and that the doctor would be in within a few minutes. As we waited on the doctor to show face, Totta and I looked at each other in a sexual way. I wanted to do something that I never had before—fuck in the examination room.

"Go head with that shit, Jonzella," he laughed at he caught on to what I was suggesting with my eyes.

"Why not?" I voiced as I opened my legs.

Laughing, he replied, "Mane, that woman can come in at any moment and catch me up in that pussy."

"Oh, the big bad Totta is scared of getting caught," I joked as a knock sounded on the door.

"See," he voiced while laughing and pointing at the door.

Rolling my eyes at him, I said, "Come in."

As my gynecologist entered the room, we spoke before she became acquainted with my current health status. Briefly looking over my folder, a series of questions were asked. Once she was done questioning me, she began to check my breasts and uterus.

"Are you having any unusual symptoms?" she inquired while lightly mashing my left titty.

"No. Is anything wrong?" I inquired curiously as I gave her my undivided attention.

"Oh no. Everything is fine. Your body is doing exactly what it supposed to at sixteen weeks," she stated as she stopped fondling my breast.

"Is my belly a little too small to be sixteen weeks?"

"No. Every woman is different. You will have some that are huge at sixteen weeks, and others that are like you," she voiced as she placed the heart monitor on my belly.

The moment she turned on the device, the sound of life filled the room. I was smiling brightly while it looked like Totta was about to faint.

"Baby, are you okay?" I asked him, trying not to giggle.

"I'm fine," he replied weakly as the gynecologist stated that our baby had a strong heartbeat.

As she cleaned off my belly, she told us that she would see me back in four weeks.

"When will we know the sex of the baby?" Totta inquired.

"Next visit," she replied with a smile on her face.

"Okay."

"You two have a lovely day," she announced before leaving the room.

"You as well," we replied in unison before she closed the door.

Placing my eyes on Totta, I asked, "What were you thinking when you heard our baby's heartbeat?"

Helping me into my pants, he said, "I'm just astonished at the little person that we made and will be responsible for until he or she is eighteen."

"Are you scared?" I asked as he slipped my coral sweater over my head.

"I ain't gon' lie to you…a little. I mean, I'm new to all of this. I've never really been around kids long enough to know what the hell to do," he voiced as I placed my feet on the ground.

Standing in front of him, I grabbed his hands and looked deeply into his eyes before saying, "We will be just fine. We got this."

"Of course we do. With a mother and sisters like mine, we will be just fine," he voiced sincerely as we exited the examination room.

After we retrieved my next appointment date card, we made our way out of the building—smiling and strolling like the happy couple that we were. That was, until we saw the same detective that approached Totta a week ago, standing in behind Totta's vehicle. Ignoring the man, Totta walked me towards the passenger side of his car.

After I was safely inside, I heard the detective say, "I'm surprised that you haven't skipped town yet. We are close to getting you arrested. I just wanted you to know that. You will soon be a ward of the state. I hope you have saved some money to give to your pregnant lady."

Totta's mental was great because he didn't say a thing to the man. He simply smiled at him. I opened the door for him, as a lady should for her man. Before he took a seat, the detective continued fucking with Totta.

"Say, all the suspect things that's going on with you and Erica can be erased if you can tell me who this big time Queenpin I keep hearing about is."

Trying my best to keep my facial expression blank, I glared at the two men.

Instantly, Totta started laughing and said, "Dude, get the fuck out of my face with that bullshit."

"You are a thug...I'm very sure you don't want to go--," he continued until Totta cut him off.

As Totta growled, my man retrieved his cell phone and pressed the number three. In a matter of seconds, the line began to ring.

Shortly, a deep voice stated, "Attorney Price."

With his eyes on the detective, Totta slid into the driver's seat as he said, "Hey, Attorney Price, this is Joshua Nixon. I need you to file charges against Detective Lorson for harassment."

"Is he in your presence as we speak?" the lawyer inquired, curiously.

"Yes."

"Where are you?"

"In front of my girlfriend's doctor's office."

"Wow. I'm on it as we speak. Hold on for a second, Mr. Nixon," Attorney Price stated as he began talking to someone else.

As I listened to the conversation, I realized that Totta's lawyer was talking to Detective Lorson's boss. Upon the funky ass detective hearing his boss's voice, he left Totta's car without a word or a glance his way.

Totta closed the door at the same time his attorney told the detective's boss that he was filing charges against his employee for harassment. They began to argue. Totta didn't move the car until his attorney had things settle with Detective Lorson's boss. After hearing that the man would be held responsible for his actions, Totta started the engine on his whip.

"Where are we going for lunch?" he asked me while reversing.

"It doesn't matter to me."

Ring. Ring. Ring.

Pulling my phone out of my purse, I saw Jonsey's name displaying across the screen.

Quickly answering the phone, I said, "Hello, sissy."

"Hey," she replied quietly.

"What's wrong with you?" I asked as I feared the worst.

"I may be having a miscarriage," she replied, trying not to cry.

"Wait, how? You haven't been complaining about no bleeding or cramping. So, where does a miscarriage come into play?" I inquired, curiously.

"I started slightly bleeding this morning. I didn't want you to worry," she said sadly.

Immediately, my heart sank for her. She was coming around to being a mom; the last thing I knew she wanted was to lose the pregnancy she was starting to love.

"What did the doctor say?" I voiced as Totta looked at me.

"That she needs to do an ultrasound and blood test first to see, and if I am having a miscarriage, there isn't anything that she can do. I would have to rest and pray for the best," her shaky tone stated in a quiet timbre.

"Is Casey with you?"

"Yes."

"Where are y'all?"

"At my doctor's office. We are waiting to have an ultrasound done."

"Okay. Totta and I are on our way."

"No. Go on about your day. I will call you once we leave here. They are calling my name. Gotta go. I love you," she voiced quickly.

"Okay. I love you more," I replied before we ended the call.

Sighing heavily, I placed my phone back into my purse.

Totta looked at me and asked, "Where is Jonsey's doctor's office at?"

"On Taylor Road, not far from A.U.M.," I voiced as I hoped that Jonsey wasn't on the verge of losing the pregnancy.

"Her and the baby will be fine, Jonzella. No need in neither of you getting worked over. Okay?"

Not sure what to think, I simply replied, "Yeah, they will be fine."

CHAPTER 18
Casey

"You okay?" I asked Jonsey as she tossed and turned in her bed.

"Yes, I just can't get comfortable," she replied calmly.

Pulling her towards me, I placed several kisses on her forehead as I rubbed her growing belly. Sliding towards her little swollen stomach, I said a silent prayer and sent up several thank you's to the Man above for my lady not having a miscarriage. As I gently rubbed her stomach, she massaged my head; all the while looking at me.

"It's weird how the body works, huh?" she questioned, closing her eyes.

"Very," I responded as I thought about the conversation the doctor had with us.

She couldn't explain why Jonsey bled. It wasn't implantation bleeding; she was quick to inform us of that. All the doctor could say was that some females bleed during their pregnancy while others don't. Yet, it was strange because Jonsey hadn't bled since that one day. I stopped worrying about it since I knew that our child was fine.

"Are you go--," she began to say until my phone started ringing.

Grabbing my phone off the pillow, she handed it to me. Seeing J-Money's name on the screen, I sighed sharply before answering the phone.

"Yo'."

"What's happening?" he asked.

"Shit. Coolin' with my lady. What's good?"

"We hitting Club Freeze tonight. Be at my crib at ten. We leaving out at ten thirty. Y'all riding with us," he stated as he inhaled.

"A'ight."

"Have you talked to that fool, Totta?"

"Yeah, earlier this morning...what's up?"

"I called that nut several times before I called you. He didn't answer the phone. I didn't leave a message so will you pass it along?"

Chuckling, I replied, "A'ight. He laid up with his ole lady. So, you know what time it is. He ain't too pleased about the latest time I interrupted them for a cell phone charger."

Busting out laughing, J-Money said, "Dude, you be on some humbug shit. Why in the hell you did that?"

"Because I love seeing that ancient black nigga get upset over some dumb shit that I do."

"I gots to get the scoop on that from him tonight," he laughed.

"I will make sure I am out of the way. He might try to fuck me up, big time," I chuckled as I heard Jonzella's door opening, followed by Totta singing.

I couldn't hold in my laughter and neither could Jonsey. J-Money wanted to know what we were laughing at so I put him on speakerphone as I hopped off the bed. Opening the door, I stuck my arm out of the door.

"Dank, go on with that fuck shit. I'm righteously tired of your ass now. I swear you can't act like a grown ass man!" Totta voiced in an annoyed timbre.

Jonsey, Jonzella, J-Money, and I laughed until Totta slammed the bathroom door.

"Casey, you better leave my man alone!" Jonzella yelled while laughing.

"I swear y'all play too damn much," J-Money voiced as he continued laughing.

"It's all love over this way. Aye, J-Money, we'll be in place tonight" I voiced, clearly ending that our conversation was at an end.

"Bet," he voiced before the call.

As I shoved my phone in my black gym shorts, I knocked on the bathroom door.

"Go away, Dank. You be on that shit, mane," Totta announced loudly.

"I ain't on no shit this time. It's business tonight at Club Freeze. We are to meet up at J-Money's crib at ten."

"A'ight," he voiced before I waltzed back into Jonsey's room.

Closing her bedroom door, I said, "So, when are we going to look for baby clothes and things of that nature."

"In another month or so. Why?" she inquired before throwing a handful of cheese cubes in her mouth.

"Just wanted to know," I voiced as I placed my body on the bed.

"Have you made the announcement to your folks that you are going to be a daddy?"

I shook my head.

With a frown on her face, she asked, "Why not?"

"Don't know," I told her honestly.

"So when are you going to do it?" she asked with a raised eyebrow.

"Soon."

Propping on her elbow, she said, "How soon?"

"This weekend," I lied, not sure if I would be in town; however, I had to get her out of my hair. I didn't want an argument over nothing.

"Okay. Am I going to be present when you tell them?"

"I would prefer for you to be," I told her honestly. My statement seemed to calm down the attitude I knew was lurking to come out of her.

"Jonsey, I might be out of town for some days. There will be times I won't be able to answer my phone, so I need you to understand that nothing is more important to me than you and our child's well-being."

"Why wouldn't you be able to answer your phone, Casey?" she inquired calmly.

That was when I knew she didn't have a clue about the street life. Immediately, I loved the woman I had gotten pregnant. She was so innocent, and that was what I needed—pure innocence so that I could leave the lifestyle behind.

For the next twenty minutes, I broke down to Jonsey what I would be doing, and how I had to be on my toes at all times. She was not thrilled about what I had to do. Quickly, I reminded her that a favor for a favor was how I lived. I had to honor what I said I was going to do; if I backed out of it, who knows what would happen to her and Jonzella. Plus, we needed the cash since I was pulling away from the street life. I sure as hell wasn't going to get a nine to five. I was going to invest my money into my own organization. What was it going to be? I sure as hell didn't know.

***

No matter where they went, Ruger and Rondon would always be front security as J-Money, Baked, DB, and Silky Snake would be behind X. Totta and I were the last ones behind The Savage Clique. There was no breaking of their formation or trying to cop a feel on the Queenpin; fuck around and get your brains blown out. Everyone knew once The Savage Clique get in single file line to move the fuck out of the way.

When we stepped inside of Club Freeze, the crowd parted as we strolled through the noisy club. Females waved and blew kisses at us; as the men were ogling X. Of course, we carried on about our business as if we didn't see them being thirsty for an ounce of our time. The way they showed us love had a nigga feeling like he was a part of a royal family. Yet, I couldn't see myself having to deal with people in my space every time they saw my face. Honestly, I didn't know how The Savage Clique dealt with that shit. It would've been drove me crazy.

The DJ mixed in one of Project Pat's songs off his Cheese and Dope 2 album. Everyone, minus Ruger, bopped their heads while rapping along. X was so into the song that it took Rondon and Ruger to ensure that nobody touched her. Her vibe alone had the club on one-thousand. It was amazing seeing how people reacted to her enjoying dancing and the music.

The Savage Clique had a bond out of this world; I pondered for so long how in the hell didn't anyone fold on her. It didn't take me long to figure out why they didn't fold on her. X broke bread with all her peoples, even the extended crew members. She didn't short anyone on their money. She took care of her people and put them on licks that she didn't want. I had to admit that she was an extraordinary, yet, a rare type of individual. People secretly hated on her, but those same haters admired her as well. She did shit, successfully, that niggas before her tried to do. It was as if she was meant to be a queenpin.

The club went crazy as the DJ played one of Boosie's songs. It was a well-known song; thus, I was rapping the words.

All I heard around me was, "I feel like I been betrayed!"

Stopping at the bar, we retrieved the buckets upon buckets filled with ice and beer. Ruger and Rondon had two large bottles of Grey Goose in their hands as we made our way to the south end of the club. No money was exchanged since X secretly owned the club. I learned of that key information tonight as we were on our way to the joint.

As we strolled through the packed club, I noticed that damn near every bitch in the joint was half naked. Thirsty niggas with blunts, bottles, and cups in their hands were lurking after the females. Chuckling to myself, I was glad that I wasn't one of those thirsty niggas that chased behind a club hopping bitch. Hell, those hoes chased after me.

The rap music ceased. I guess the DJ was tired of niggas throwing up gang signs and bouncing around like fools, causing him to amp the females up by playing a twerking jam. Ass and titties began bouncing as the movement towards the back of the club came to a halt. Peeking around Silky Snake's tall body frame, I had to see why we stopped moving.

Ooouu, shit! My God. Dank, get yo' eyes away from that woman shaking her ass like that, I thought as I tried to keep my eyes from watching her ass jiggle and wiggle.

X was twerking so motherfucking great that she had niggas and bitches making it rain in the joint. I couldn't lie as if she didn't know how to throw that ass because she did. I couldn't lie as if the thought of her fucking like she danced didn't come across my mind. If I wasn't in my right mind, I would've been tried to holler at her slim-thick ass.

As every person's eyes in the vicinity were locked in on X, I noticed that Totta's eyes lingered in a particular area too long, which meant that he saw someone that he didn't know very well but had seen before.

Clearing my throat, I waited until he came to me with what was on his mind.

Shortly afterwards, Totta turned to me. I placed my ear to his mouth to ensure that he spoke to me at once. As Totta spoke in my ear, I saw X dancing with Rondon. Instantly, I assumed there was something going on between them; yet, I knew they weren't that stupid to mix business and pleasure together. A good bit of shit Totta was saying I didn't fully hear since I had my own thoughts going on. However, one statement my partner whispered in my ear stayed on my mind.

Once X finished dancing, she motioned for Ruger and Rondon to get in front of her. Before walking off, Totta quickly looked at me. I pointed in front of him, signalling for him to catch up. The last thing I needed to do was acknowledge that I was ready to tear the motherfucking club up!

After he mouthed okay, he began to stroll behind DB.

As I walked behind Totta, all I could think about was his statement, *"You see that nigga that's standing behind that nigga in all-white? That's the nigga that came looking for Jonsey."*

My mind kept replaying what Totta said to me. The more I thought about that ugly ass fuck nigga coming to my girl's crib, the more I became angry. However, at the moment, I couldn't get down and dirty. Business with the most important woman in the world was underway, and nothing or no one was going to stop what we had to conduct.

On life, I'mma make it my business to keep my eyes on that fuck nigga. Ain't no motherfucking way in hell I'mma let the nigga slide. Whatever he thinking gon' cease the moment I step down on his ass. If he don't like what I have to say, then he will receive a well whooped ass. One damn thing I know for certain, Jonsey Brown is all mine, I thought as we made our way towards the back of the building.

Halfway towards the meeting spot, I felt a strong tug. Turning around to see who in the hell had the audacity to touch me, I saw Diamond's ugly ass smiling as she showcased a bottom row of gold teeth. Standing tall in a pink halter top, mini-skirt outfit, Diamond looked like a weird creature from a fucking safari.

With a smirk on my face, I strolled away. I be damned if the broad didn't tug on me harder followed by coming closer to me.

After I snatched her ass towards me, I whispered in her ear, "Look, stay away from me. I ain't in the mood to be fucking with you, guh. It's over. There shouldn't be a reason you are approaching me in the first place."

"I still want you," she cooed.

Laughing, I walked off on the bitch; only for her to shove my head forwards. Before I could gain my composure, I turned around and slapped the shit out of her. Some niggas around me got mad and started to walk towards Diamond and me. Instantly, they stopped in their tracks. I didn't have to turn around to know who was standing behind me. X crept in front of me and glared at Diamond.

Shortly afterwards, X motioned for Diamond to come to her. Like the weak bitch that she was, Diamond was inches away from the lovely dressed X. Placing her mouth to Diamond's ear, X whispered something in my ex's ear. Immediately, Diamond threw up her hands and looked at me. Apologizing as she backed away, I had a frown on my face as to what X said to her. I tried to inquire, but X mouthed that it was meeting time. While we travelled towards the back of the club, I pondered what in the hell did X tell Diamond. A nigga was hoping that she would tell me soon as the meeting was over.

As soon as she took a seat in a chair, followed by Ruger standing behind, the meeting was under way. Halfway through, I realized that I couldn't wait to leave the damn club. I wanted to be underneath my lady while watching TV or eating a meal.

"So, the work will be in no later than five days. Totta and Dank, y'all will be making drops throughout this state, Mississippi, and Georgia. Y'all will not move the dope in one jug. You will move to the southern parts of Alabama, one weekend. Followed by being in the northern parts the next weekend. After that weekend, you will be in Mississippi. Soon as you leave Mississippi, you will go straight to Georgia. Y'all will be in Georgia for at least two weeks.

Once all the dope is distributed to the assigned places, then the favor is completed. Any questions?" she inquired as she looked amongst Totta and me.

"No," we replied in unison.

"Good," she stated before going into another topic that had nothing to do with Totta and me.

An hour later, the meeting ended, and I was happy as fuck. The music, club hoppers, and the smell of cigarettes and weed were getting on my nerves. Unbeknownst to me, none of The Savage Clique members or Totta wanted to be in Club Freeze.

In the back of the line as we ambled towards the front door, I felt eyes on me. Looking around the packed out club, I couldn't see a set of eyes on me. Halfway towards the door, the fuck nigga that came looking for my lady approached me, from the left side.

"So, you the nigga fucking my ex-bitch, huh?" he chuckled as he blew smoke in my face.

There was no response as I slammed my fists into the nigga's face. We went blow for blow. He popped me a couple of times, and I brought the thunder on that nigga's head. I had to whoop the dog shit out of ole boy. He was a disrespectful bastard that needed to be taught some manners. He had the wrong Alabama nigga fucked up if he thought he was going to come at me sideways about my woman. Nawl, my folks didn't raise no bitch ass nigga!

Once I had his mouth leaking, I put my mouth to his ear and growled, "Jonsey is mine. The next time you come her way...that's your motherfucking ass, my nigga. I kill niggas for the fuck of it."

Walking away from the fuck nigga, I knew that Jonsey was going to let me chat with her father. That nigga and I had some shit that we had to discuss. I was close to getting away from the street life, and no one was going to place me back in it once I called it quits.

CHAPTER 19
Jonsey

Jonzella and I were having a grand time as we chatted, ate popcorn, and enjoyed several movies. All of that changed the moment, she got a call from Totta stating that Casey had been shot. Instantly, the color in my face drained as my heart raced. While throwing the covers off us, Jonzella tried to tell me to be calm, yet, I couldn't. I feared the worst as I had thousands of questions slamming into my mental.

"Will you slow down before you hurt yourself?" she stated as I quickly dressed followed by running out of my room.

"What hospital he at?" I asked as she ran towards her room.

"Jackson," she responded loudly as I watched her throw on a pair of pants.

As I snatched my keys off the key holder, Jonzella was running down the hallway, shouting, "Don't you get in the driver's seat of your car. I'm driving."

Not acknowledging her, I ran towards my car. As soon as I unlocked the door, I hopped in the passenger seat. I knew I shouldn't be behind the wheel in the current state that I was. As my driver's door opened, I slammed the key into the ignition, followed by turning the key over.

"Pam" by USDA blasted from the speakers. Jonzella giggled as I didn't see anything funny.

With a weird facial expression, I asked, "What's so funny?"

"You listening to this CD," she replied as she reversed my whip.

"Casey had to have put it in," I stated while fumbling with his hands.

In my pocket, my cell phone vibrated. Quickly, I grabbed my phone. Seeing Casey's name on the screen, I held my breath as I answered the phone.

"Aye, baby. I know Jonzella told you what happened. Don't be worrying and stressing yourself and our baby out. I'm good. The bullet just grazed my arm. They are patching it up now. We should be up out--," he stated before I cut him off.

"We are on our way up there. You know good and well you can't tell me not to worry. I love you, so you know it's in my nature to worry about you," I told him as I felt relieved that there wasn't any major damage done.

Chuckling, he replied, "Well, I'm in triage eight. I love you, Ms. Lady."

With a smile on my face, I replied, "And Ms. Lady loves you, Eleven Golds."

Ending the call, I looked at Jonzella and said, "Hurry up and get me to my man."

Laughing, she replied, "You act like we live hella far from the hospital. It's literally down the dang road. You heard him say that he is okay, and not to worry. So, you need to do just that."

Before she could park my car good enough, I hopped out— running toward the entrance of the emergency room. Upon entering the hospital, I saw a sea of faces that I didn't know. All types of shapes, sizes, and multi-colored weave wearing females were chatting as they waited on a loved one. Instantly, I wondered how many people got shot tonight, and what the hell happened for a shooting to take place.

"Hmph, what she doing here?" I heard a bitch say, who was sitting close to the women's bathroom.

"Who you talking about, Diamond?" another female chimed.

Instantly, I knew who the bitch was that had the audacity to question why I was at the hospital, but didn't have the balls to answer the other female's question.

Placing my eyes on her, I rubbed my belly and said, "Let me go check on my man."

Jonzella knew what type of shit I was on; thus, she laughed. As we waltzed towards the security guards, Diamond had some slick shit to say. For the sake of my unborn child, I didn't entertain the bitch.

She was going to see what it was the moment Casey and I strolled out of the emergency room—hand in hand.

Before we got a chance to tell the security guard where we needed to go, Casey and Totta strolled out, talking. Upon seeing us, they ambled towards us. Casey looked so damn good in his attire, which consisted of all-black with a touch of gray. His black and gray A hat was cocked to the right. The gold in his mouth, around his neck, and wrists had my pussy percolating. His entire bad boy persona was doing a number on me, and I was ready to fuck and be fucked!

"Aye, Dank, you good, woe?" a female inquired from behind me.

As he stepped closer to me, I turned to see what bitch was asking my man about his health. My mouth dropped the moment I saw a gorgeous, cinnamon brown woman, with a bottom gold grill, big brown eyes, flawless skin, and a nicely shaped body looking our way as she had six burly, dark-skinned, fine ass niggas with her.

While wrapping his left arm around my swollen waist, he replied, "Yeah, I'm good. Y'all good?"

As the group of unknown individuals nodded their head, it seemed as if they glided towards us. Once they were in close range, they did their dap thing with Totta and Casey.

"Get you some rest. J-Money will be in contact with y'all," the woman stated in a tone only we could hear.

"A'ight," Casey and Totta replied in unison as someone, that I knew very well, yelled some shit that had me shaking in my boots.

"Whoever capped my motherfucking homie, Demante...gonna get the business. On life, we ain't leaving until whoever murked my nigga, get the same fate!" It was Demante's right hand man, Jox.

I was scared to look him in the face; thus, I kept my eyes on Casey.

Placing a kiss on my forehead, Casey whispered, "You don't have shit to worry about. I ain't going nowhere, and ain't naan nigga or his crew going to fuck with you or me. That's on my life."

"I see that we should be leaving before I show my natural black ass," the female hissed.

"What you wanna do about that nigga capping his mouth?" one of her burly guys inquired.

"Let him make a fool out of himself. I'm in the mood to fuck, so I guess we are going to call it an early night," she informed her crew before telling us to have a good night.

When the chick and her goons began walking, so did we. As we moved behind them, it seemed as if everyone in the waiting room stopped talking and watched us walk away. Instantly, I knew that the female we were walking behind was possibly the same chick that had my father shook. I made a mental note that the moment we were in my car, I was going to ask Casey who she was.

Before we made it to the door good enough, Diamond said, "These hoes love saying they are pregnant for a nigga and ain't a bit more pregnant than the man on the moon."

The chick and her crew stopped, which caused us to stop walking. The four guys in the back stepped to the side where we could see the voluptuous ass on the bossy female.

She didn't turn her head as she nastily said, "Diamond, like I told yo' ass in the club. Bite down off Dank. He don't want you. Let that shit go. You cause any issues with him, and I promise you...I'mma beat the brakes off yo' ass. Stay in a child's place when grown folks are in your presence, little girl."

There wasn't anything else to be said; thus, the chick and her goons resumed walking.

As we strolled behind them, the chick yelled out, "Dank, if you have any more troubles out of that bitch, please let me know. She really testing me, and I don't like to be tested."

With a serious facial expression, he replied, "A'ight."

"Oh by the way, Totta," she voiced as the four guys behind her moved out the way while she spun on her heels.

"What's up?" Totta voiced as we stopped inches away from the powerful crew.

Since there were people strolling towards us, she chuckled before speaking in a low tone, "You did a fine job yesterday."

With a crazy facial expression, I wanted to know what in the hell was she talking about.

Apparently, Totta did as well because he asked, "What are you talking about?"

"You were tested yesterday at the doctor's office," she voiced with a hint of laughter.

Shaking his head while laughing, he said, "No disrespect but you ain't shit for that one."

"I just gotta know who I'm dealing with. I needed to know whether you going to fold if pressure was applied to your neck," she stated seriously.

Nodding his head, he responded with, "I was built for pressure."

"To deal with me, y'all gotta be built for the pressure." Her statement caused the males to laugh.

"With that being said, that lil' situation you "were" a suspect in will be gone within forty-eight hours. She will no longer be messing with you and your girl."

"Thank you," he replied, sincerely.

With a pleasant smile on her face, she sweetly replied, "I should be the one thanking y'all. I truly thank y'all for the talk we had some nights ago. Now, go home and rest up."

"No problem. You have a good night, woman," Totta and Dank replied in unison.

"Same to y'all."

As we parted ways from the powerful woman and her crew, several questions slammed into my brain. I couldn't wait until we were distant from them before I said a word. In two minutes, we arrived at my car. Jonzella hopped in the driver's seat as I told Totta that he could sit in the passenger seat.

"Thanks," he replied as I opened the back door for Casey.

"No problem," I voiced as I slide in, beside my man.

As Jonzella started the engine, Totta asked, "Aye, Dank, do you want to leave your whip at J-Money's crib or do you want us to go get it?"

"I'm in the mood to ride before we turn in. Let's go scoop it up," he stated as he leaned his head on my shoulder.

"A'ight," he replied to my man.

After Totta told Jonzella to jump on the interstate as if she was going to Eastdale Mall, I decided to ask the questions that were in my head.

"So, Casey, who was that chick and the dudes she was with?"

"They are the people y'all father is scared of," he stated casually.

"Should we be worried about them?" I inquired as Jonzella's heavy foot ass smashed the gas pedal.

"Nope. As long as Totta and I do our jobs correctly, y'all will have no issues out of them."

"Okay," I quickly stated before continuing, "How in the world did she rise to be so powerful?"

Totta cleared his throat. I didn't know what that meant but I kept my eyes on my man as I waited for the answer.

"Because she was determined."

"Oh," I replied, ending the topic.

"What happened at the club?" Jonzella asked, glancing at Totta.

"That fuck nigga that came to the house looking for Jonsey stepped to Dank the wrong way. A fight took place between them. Bruh wore that nigga ass out, and he didn't like that. We was getting ready to leave and that fool Demante ran to a car and pulled out a gun, which resulted in a shootout in the club's parking lot," Totta stated as he reclined my seat backwards.

"Is Demante dead?" I heard my small voice ask.

"Yep. His body was riddled with quite a few bullets," Totta responded before laughing.

Looking at Casey, I quickly kissed the top of his forehead. He was dozing off, and I wasn't going to disturb him while he was resting. The car grew quiet as Jonzella followed the directions that Totta gave her. It didn't take us long to reach a quiet yet beautiful neighborhood. The community was well lit; thus, I could see that each yard had manicured grass and perfectly trimmed bushes.

There were no toys in the front yard nor a late model or raggedy car were parked in the drive way.

As Jonzella pulled onto the curb of a large home with a massive front yard, I saw my man's car parked behind a gray, old school Monte Carlo.

"Are y'all hungry?" Totta asked before opening the passenger door.

"Yep. Waffle House," we replied in unison.

In a matter of seconds, we burst into laughter because my sleeping boyfriend was quick to answer about being hungry.

"Look at Lazarus," Totta chuckled before shaking his head.

"Jonzella, get everybody's order, then call me. Take him to the crib, he needs some rest," Totta demanded before exiting the car.

Leaving the well-put together community, I slipped off into La-La-Land as I thought about Demante being killed miles away from home. I didn't feel bad about him not living; yet, I didn't want any karma coming Casey's or Totta's way for protecting me. Immediately, I began to pray for their safety.

When I finished praying, Jonzella's cell phone rang. Apparently, it was Totta by the way she answered the phone. Once she told him what she wanted to eat, I told her to double her order. Casey's ass had to do the most when it came down to his order. All I could do was laugh and shake my head. He was eating as if he was the one pregnant. After Jonzella ended the call with Totta, her mobile device rang again. This time her tone was different when she said hello.

"Yes, Daddy, we are fine," she voiced lightly as she hopped in the fast lane and drove the hell out of my car.

"How do you know what happened?" she inquired, curiously.

The scoff noise she made informed me that Renee or someone else she didn't like was mentioned.

"Nothing, Daddy," my sister voiced in an agitated timbre.

"All I'm saying is that I don't want anything to do with Renee. Will you please stop pushing her off on me? She made her choice, and I've made--," my sister stated before stopping her sentence.

Apparently, Dad had nipped her statement in the bud to stand up for Renee's sorry ass.

"No, I don't want a DNA test done. Daddy, I don't care to know if you are my biological father or not. It doesn't matter. You have always been there, and no test will have to prove to me that you are my father."

"I love you more," she responded softly as she hopped onto Perry Hill Road exit.

"How's Mom doing?"

The pause from Jonzella made me worry a bit, but then I realized that my mother didn't need me to worry about her ruthless ass. I had to check my feelings about the woman that gave birth to me. No more feeling sorry for a woman that let her husband murder their children, or didn't have the balls to leave him.

"What do you mean...you believe she's having a psychotic break?" Jonzella's high pitched timbre sounded off.

"Do you need for us to come up and help you?" she inquired.

You must be planning on going up there by yourself. I'm done with those sneaky fuckers, I thought while rubbing the side of Casey's face.

"May I speak with her?"

In a split second, Jonzella whined, "But why not, Daddy. Maybe her hearing my voice will bring her out of whatever she has going on."

"Okay," she replied before ending the call as she made a left turn on Harrison Road.

Out of curiosity, I asked, "What is going on up there?"

"Daddy said that Mother is losing her mind. Rocking back and forth while staring off into space, then she would have a full conversation with herself. He thinks she's having a breakdown of some sort."

"Yeah, a breakdown from being a low-down individual," I hissed.

"You don't know that she had anything to do with Kevin and Kenny's deaths," Jonzella stated in a defensive manner.

"Sister, sister, I'm afraid that we don't know the people that raised us."

CHAPTER 20
Totta

Saturday, April, 15th

The past two weeks had been hell for Dank and me. We hadn't been home since we got word that it was time for us to make our delivers. Our first route outside of Alabama was to Memphis, Tennessee; afterwards, we were drop down inin Decatur, Georgia. Dank and I thought it was best to deliver the dope in one swoop instead of taking breaks; that way we could be done with the dope game and finish our lives the right way.

The girls wanted to start going to church on Sundays, and we were cool with that. The only way Dank and I knew how to get our lives right were to be on the same page as God intended us to be; in addition, to doing right by our ladies. I couldn't lie as if I wasn't scared of walking into someone's church after all the wrong I had done. Truth be told, I saw it as a blessing that I was able to turn my life around for the sake of my child and family. I prayed daily that I wouldn't have the same fate as those that I had killed or ordered to be killed. Before I closed my eyes at whatever hotel we were staying at, I made sure that I read the daily quote, a bible verse, and prayed.

"Aye, Totta...ain't that that nigga that X popped on his wedding day?" Casey inquired as he munched on a beef jerky and cheese snack.

"Where?" I inquired as I looked around the small shopping center.

"Standing behind that white Suburban with tinted windows," he voiced while pointing towards the front entrance of Bath and Body Works.

Placing my eyes on the group of men, I zoned into the light-skinned guy's face. I didn't know what to believe. It was highly unlikely that the guy was Bango. Yet, I couldn't be so sure.

"Dank, I highly doubt that Bango is alive. That guy was shot with an assault rifle. Folks said that his father carried him out of the wedding area with his jacket over his son's face. That guy has to be someone that looks like Bango," I stated while rolling a blunt.

"If it is him, some shit is going to pop off and we need to be the fuck out of the way," Dank informed me as he started the engine on the rental we were in.

Nodding in agreement, I kept my eyes on the guy. I paid close attention to the way he walked, held up his hand, and chatted with the Italian males around him. As I saw the gold teeth in the guy's mouth, something in my core told me that it was Bango.

"Do we call J-Money and let him know that we think Bango is alive and kicking it in Gulfport, Mississippi?" I inquired as I reached for my phone.

"Nope," he quickly stated.

"Why not?" I asked as I placed my eyes on my partner.

"Because that shit could go two ways. One, we could be told to finish that nigga off, or two, we might stir up some shit when it's not even necessary."

Sighing heavily, I replied, "A'ight."

"Plus, we don't know if that guy really is Bango. Dude look all rugged by the face and shit. Just leave that shit alone, Dank."

***

"Totta, when will you be back home?" Jonzella whined for the millionth time this week.

"I told you as soon as I can."

"I'm horny as fuckkk," she cooed as she dragged out the 'k' in the curse word.

Growling, I knew Dank and I had to hurry up and finish the favor we owed X. I hadn't had my dick wet since the night Dank got shot.

I was tired of beating my dick while in the shower. That shit wasn't doing anything for me.

"Shid, me too. Wacking off ain't doing me no justice," I sighed as I noticed my wood growing, pressing against the zipper of my jeans.

"Let's have phone sex," she moaned as I knew she was rubbing gently on her clit.

"A'ight," I voiced as I hoped like hell Dank would stay outside until Jonzella and I were done having phone sex.

Jumping off the bed, I skipped to the bathroom. As I was making my way, my phone notified me that Jonzella was requesting to video chat. Accepting the request, I quickly ambled into the bathroom.

"Damn, baby, you ready for this, ain't it?" I chuckled as I locked the bathroom door.

While moaning, Jonzella showed me her freshly shaved pussy as she slid two fingers in and out of her fat monkey.

"My God, I can't wait to get back to you," I groaned as I freed my man.

Resisting stroking my dick, I took a seat on the toilet and watched my pregnant woman play with her pussy. Jonzella continued to finger fuck her pussy until she lowly groaned in the phone.

"Let me see that sex face, baby," I groaned while licking my lips.

As soon as I saw my baby's sex face, I busted into laughter as the images of Mr. Ed the horse popped into my brain. Jonzella didn't have big teeth, but her facial expression led me to my image of that damn horse. My laughter killed the mood as my dick went flaccid.

"What in the fuck is so funny, Totta?" she yelped with a frown on her face.

"That damn sex face you just made had me thinking about Mr. Ed the horse," I laughed harder as I heard the room door closing.

"Mane, I hope you ain't stinking up the bathroom again," Dank stated as Jonzella cursed me out before ending the video chat.

Laughing as I fixed myself, Dank wanted to know what had me laughing. I couldn't respond because he didn't need to know why I was laughing so hard; hell, I could barely stop laughing.

Opening the bathroom door, he said, "Damn, you ain't going to wash your hands or nothing?"

Shaking my head, I laughed. Finally, I had my laughter under control as I plopped down on the foot of the bed.

"What in the hell is wrong with you, guy?" Dank inquired as he retrieved clothes from his suitcase.

"Mane, you don't even want to know," I lightly chuckled while shaking my head.

"Spill the beans, woe."

Once I told him what had me tickled, he busted out in laughter and said, "Mane, I had to stifle my laughter once I saw Jonsey's face. I swear that face did something to me, and not make me wanna jump off in her either."

Ring. Ring. Ring.

Looking at my phone, I knew Jonzella was hot about what took place moments ago.

"I'm finna hit the shower. Jonzella finna curse your ass out, and I don't want to witness that," he joked as I answered the phone.

The moment she heard my voice, she went in.

"So, yo' black ass wasn't going to call me back, huh?" she inquired with an attitude.

"You were in your feelings, and I didn't have time for that. So, I decided that I would wait until you came out of our feelings before dialing your digits," I replied as I lay back on the bed.

"You gon' fuck around and make me do something to you, boy," she snarled.

For the life of me, I didn't know why she had the audacity to call me a boy. That word pissed me off more than a nigga stealing from me.

"What I told yo' ass 'bout callin' me a boy, guh?"

"What yo' black ass gonna do about it?" she hissed with anger in her voice.

She was seeking an argument, and I wasn't up for her shit. I was going to end this call before we said some shit to each other.

"If you seeking an argument, you need to call me back when you get some act right."

"Nawl, I asked your ass a question, boy!" she screamed.

I didn't respond. I ended the call and powered off my phone. I wasn't going to deal with her disrespectful ass because she was horny than a motherfucker. Hell, I was too but she didn't see me going the fuck off.

Lying on the bed, I contemplated with powering on my phone so I wouldn't have hell to pay when I touched back in Montgomery. Thinking long and hard about the situation, I decided not to cut my phone back on.

"Aye, man, please cut your phone back on!" Dank yelled from the bathroom.

Ignoring him, I thought about my past. My feelings were all over the place once I thought about my first kill, followed by all the others. My thoughts were interrupted the moment Dank yelled for me to cut my cell phone on.

"No. She wanna argue, and I'm not up for that," I told him, loudly.

As I tried to resume thinking on my past, Dank opened the bathroom door. Steam left the bathroom as he waltzed out. I knew he had some shit to tell me, so I looked at him.

"Jonzella going ham because you turned your phone off."

"She'll be alright. Change of subject, please."

"What's on your mind, Totta?"

"Mane, I'm thinking about reaping what I sowed," I said honestly as I kept my eyes on him as he moved towards the bed he was occupying.

"Elaborate," he said while taking a seat.

"Mane, we killed a lot of people whether it was the dope or slicing necks or shooting them. I'm thinking will I be there to see my child become the person they supposed to be in life? Will someone try to knock me off the map like I've done plenty of niggas? Will someone try to do me the same way I did Erica? What if someone comes after Jonzella and my seed, mane? How am I supposed to react to that?"

"One thing I know, ain't a fucking soul going to fuck with you, Jonzella, your child, or your family. Yeah, we are leaving the game, but we must still be on our shit as if we are still in the game. We won't fuck with nobody that we weren't already fucking with. Ya dig?"

As I nodded my head, I had mixed feelings on what he was saying. At the end of the day, I guess I wanted a stress free life from the streets.

Ring. Ring. Ring.

"Aye, if that's Jonsey calling, tell her that I will power on my phone in a minute," I quickly stated.

"It ain't Jonsey. It's J-Money," Dank voiced quickly before answering the phone.

"A'ight," I replied as my partner answered the phone.

"Yo'," Dank spat in the phone.

As my partner chatted on the phone, I thought about my future with my woman and child. One minute the thoughts were good, and the next they weren't. My mind zoomed with several questions that left me with no answers.

What would I do if I reap what I've sown? What would I do if someone decides to roll up on me while my child is in the car with me? Should I escape the city I've been born and raised in to avoid the negative backlash that could come our way?

"Aye, Totta," Dank stated, shaking me from my thoughts.

"What's up?" I replied as I gave him my undivided attention.

"Are you sleepy?"

With a puzzled facial expression, I lifted my body off the bed while shaking my head.

"Good. Let's get up outta here. We have twelve bricks left to drop off."

With a frown on my face, I wondered why he was in a rush to leave; thus, I asked.

"Why are you rushing to leave?"

"X had an expedited order that needs to go out to Savannah, Georgia. Then, before we are officially done we have to put that pressure down on the younger niggas in the city."

"Shit, I righteously forgot about that shit," I voiced before sighing.

"Truth be told, so did I."

As we hopped from the bed, the room was silent. With so much shit going on, a brother forgot about the shit we had to do with the young niggas. I preferred to do a little killing, rather than telling them shit that they should already know about the streets.

Thirty minutes later, we were hitting the interstate heading back to X's headquarters so that we could re-up. Along the way to Alabama, I received a call from my mother stating that Danzo and two other guys bodies were found in family members trash cans.

"Shit!" Dank stated as chills ran through my body after I told him what my mother said.

"Welp, that's what happens when you go against the hand that feeds you."

"Sure is. Now is the perfect time to get out of the game. So much shit is going on that it's unbelievable. I ain't trying to get caught up in nobody's bullshit. It's time to really put our families first," Dank stated as he fired up a cigarette.

"Indeed," I replied as patted my newly purchased Newport box.

"How are we going to handle these young niggas?" I asked while pulling out a cigarette.

"Hopefully, we won't. I'm praying that the message is already received thanks to Danzo and those fuck niggas bodies being pulled out of their family members trash cans," he replied, taking a quick look my way.

"Well, let's hope that's the best solution."

CHAPTER 21
Jonzella

Thursday, April 20th

I was glad when Totta strolled through my door this morning, saying that he was done with the game. I was extremely pleased to know that he was willing to go to church with me. Everything that I had wished for in a man and relationship, I had it. Yeah, it came with a price of hurt and pain; yet, everything panned out right for me. I didn't have to stress over getting a phone call from someone telling me that Totta was in jail or dead. I was able to breathe like I did prior to dealing with Totta.

"What are you smiling about, woman?" he hissed in my ear as we were sitting at his mother's kitchen table.

"All of my prayers have been answered," I cooed as I placed a kiss on his lips.

"Many more prayers are going to get answered as long as you treat me as you have been doing," he voiced sincerely as he gently stroked my right cheek.

"Aww, ain't y'all cute," his mother stated happily as she strolled into the kitchen.

"They are very cute," his sisters stated in unison as they placed club sandwiches, chips, cookies, and a cake on the kitchen table.

Before Totta's sisters and mother took a seat at the table, they placed the rest of the finger foods on the table. Once everyone placed food onto their plates, one question sparked an intriguing conversation.

"Where are you from?" Totta's mother inquired.

"I was born and raised in Fort Lauderdale, Florida, but we moved to Prattville, Alabama for a short time. Then, we moved to Myrtle Beach, South Carolina," I voiced after I bit into a piece of my sandwich.

"How long have you been in Alabama since you've moved from Prattville?" his mother continued.

"Since I was eighteen. My sister and I came down here to attend college."

"Are you close to graduating?"

"In three years. As of next year I will be new to motherhood, so I decided that I would take a semester off in the spring."

As we made polite conversation about my degree and part of my family tree, the topic moved to their family tree and where their families originated from. While they rambled on about their family members, I knew that I couldn't have picked a better man to be the father of my child and someone I could grow old with.

"Out of all my siblings, there is one that I can't stand with a passion with her funky, no good ass," his mother growled nastily.

"Auntie Meek," Totta and his sisters replied in unison before chucking.

"Nope, not that hag. Y'all have an aunt that I have never told y'all about because she wasn't worth talking about and still ain't. Renee Johnson," she voiced before taking a sip of tea.

Instantly, I began to cough while keeping my eyes on her. I prayed like hell there was another Renee Johnson she was talking about.

"Are you okay, baby?" Totta inquired as patted my back.

Nodding my head, the hairs on my body stood as I felt nasty. Pulling out my phone, I opened my photo gallery and retrieved a picture of my birth mother. Sliding the phone towards Totta's mother, I prayed heavily as his mother looked at the screen on my phone with bucked eyes.

"Jonzella, who is this woman to you?" Totta's mother inquired with a shaky tone.

The timbre of her voice confirmed what I was praying wasn't true. I knew I was in deep, nasty shit as I learned that I was pregnant and in love with my first cousin!

"She's my biological mother," I voiced as the tears streamed down my face.

"What is going on?" Totta voiced in an alarmed tone.

Totta's mother slammed her back against the kitchen chair while shaking her head. Placing her eyes on me, the look she gave me was unexplainable. I felt my body shaking as Totta and his sisters continued to ask what was wrong.

I lifted my body from the chair as I shook my head uncontrollably.

"Will someone say something to me, damn it!" Totta voiced angrily.

"Y'all remember me telling y'all that I have a niece somewhere in this world, and I didn't know her name or her whereabouts?" I heard his mother say as I felt my knees growing weak.

"Mane, y'all better be playing a damn joke on me or something. I know damn well you ain't finna tell me that Jonzella is my damn cousin!" he yelped.

"I'm sorry, son. She is your first cousin," I heard her say.

The sound that came from his mouth crippled me as I began to drop towards the floor. Totta's mother caught me before I landed on the floor.

Rubbing my shoulders, I couldn't look Totta in his face as he snarled, "What kind of fuck shit is this?"

I could tell that he was royally pissed and disgusted; by the way he was talking told it all. The things he was saying informed me that he was truly hurt by hearing a complete lie. I hate to cease the nasty prank that his mother and I conjured as payback for him eating up her cookies. Glancing up at his mother, I busted out in laughter as well as she did.

Beyond tickled, we crashed on the floor as he asked, "What in the hell so funny?"

"You, nigga," his mother stated while laughing.

"Mom, was that a prank you and Jonzella did on him?" one of his sisters inquired.

As we nodded our heads, Totta went off. It took his mother getting stern with him for him to cease his attitude towards us.

"I bet you will fly straight from here on out," she laughed as she took a seat at the table.

"So, who's idea was it to prank me like that?" he inquired, looking between his mother and me.

"It was my idea," she stated as she raised her hands.

Shaking his head, he looked at me and asked, "So, you are not my cousin?"

"Nope," I smiled while rubbing the side of his face.

"Mane, y'all play too much," he quickly voiced before continuing, "Jonzella, I got you, woman."

"And I'm looking forward to it," I chuckled as his mother and I gave each other a hi-five.

We finished our lunch on a great note, followed by watching a movie. Once we finished the movie, his sisters, mother, and I chatted while he handled some business on his phone. I enjoyed being around his family; they were down-to-earth and loving people. I was glad that my unborn child would have wonderful aunts and grandmother.

An hour later, Totta appeared in the front room with an ugly look upon his face. The type of look that informed me shit wasn't good on his end. On the ride to his crib, Totta was silent as hell. I tried talking to him, but he gave me the silent treatment. I didn't like that one bit. The only way I knew to get him out of the quiet zone was to give him some bomb as head.

Pulling out his dick and shoving it in my mouth, I gobbled my man's dick as if my life depended on it. As I was doing my thing with a mouthful of dick, I was disappointed that I didn't get the reaction I wanted from him; however, I continued going—that was, until I couldn't take him showing no emotions or making any sounds. Removing my mouth from his dick, I angrily shoved it in his boxers.

"Thank you," he stated with sarcasm.

Pushing his head, I asked, "So, you gonna act like that with me?"

"Nawl. Got a lot on my mind," he voiced as I noticed he wasn't going to his apartment.

"Where are we going, and what's on your mind?"

"We riding to Hope Hull," he voiced in a blank tone.

"Totta, talk to me."

"Not until I have my thoughts together."

Knowing damn well that I was talking to a brick wall, I sat back in the seat and tried my best to get him to talk to me. I had to give up because he refused to talk to me.

Moments later, Totta hopped off the highway and zoomed down a bumpy, country road of Hope Hull.

As he passed a set of bushes, he paid close attention to the area, which made me ask him, "What is so special about those bushes?"

"That's where I dumped Erica's body at."

Chills ran through me the moment he spoke. It wasn't what he said; it was how he said it. If I didn't know any better, I would've sworn that there was a hidden message in his comment. There was a reason why he brought me on a lonely, ugly road; yet, I sure as hell wasn't going to ask. Placing my hand on my belly, I began to pray that whatever was on Totta's mind that he would find the solution.

Turning onto a dirt road, Totta slowly drove up the red, rocky gravel. I became antsy as I wondered what in the hell were we doing in this area. I guess he saw me fidgeting with a questionable expression upon my face.

Chuckling, he said, "Are you scared, my lady?"

"No," I lied while looking at my surroundings.

"Good, you shouldn't be. I won't do anything to you," he voiced as he brought his car to a halt.

Shoving the gearshift in the park position, Totta ordered for me to get out of the car. I didn't want to get out; however, I had no choice. Slowly removing the seatbelt from my body, I opened the car door. My breathing was erratic as I moved at a snail's pace away from the passenger seat. I was startled the moment he slammed the driver's door.

"Come on, woman. I ain't finna do anything to you that you don't deserve," he growled, which brought fear towards my heart.

Strolling towards the back of his car, I held his gaze. He was emotionless as he stood with his right hand held out, a smirk on his face, and a strong body posture.

As I approached him, I wanted to know what he was going to do to me and why. Nearing him, Totta roughly pulled me towards him only to shove me against the back of his car.

His soft, yet manly left hand caressed the side of my face while he gently rubbed my right hand, all the while glaring into my eyes. Dropping my shaky right hand, Totta began to unbuckle my belt, followed by unbuttoning my shorts. In a flash, my shorts and panties were shoved to the ground, all the while with Totta glaring into my eyes.

Being the beast that I knew he could be, Totta roughly spread my legs, followed by closely eyeing my pussy before slamming his mouth on my hot twat. Feeling his warm, extremely moist mouth along with the vibrations from him humming, caused my head to fly backwards as a high groan escaped my lips. As I enjoyed the roughness of Totta's oral sex skills, my body began to shake the moment he slapped my thigh.

"Ahh!" I cooed as he continued attacking the one place I loved for him to be near.

While my killer of a man servicing my lady, he slid me onto the trunk of his car. My legs were spread as wide as they could go. My belly was protruding the more I was close to climaxing. With a rigid body, a soaking wet pussy, and a loud whimper, I was ready to blast off in Totta's mouth. That was, until he removed his mouth from my pussy.

"Why are you stopping?" I cooed as I glared at him.

Not speaking a word to me, Totta gazed at me with an emotionless facial expression while undressing himself from head to toe. Once he was stark naked, he proceeded to take off my shirt and bra. The sun was beating down on us as we were on the verge of having sex in the wooded area of an unknown place.

With his dick inches away from my pussy, Totta roughly grabbed a fistful of my hair. Shoving my head towards his, he sucked on my bottom lip. He bit my lip, and I whimpered from the pain. I didn't know what he had on his mind, but I knew I had to tell him to be gentle with me.

"You are being a bit rough, Totta," I said softly as the head of his dick touched my clit, causing me to rotate my lower region just to feel the wonderful sensation.

Grabbing my hair tighter and slamming his dick inside of me, Totta nastily said, "Shut the fuck up and take whatever I give you."

Shocked at the way he talked to me, I wanted to protest but I couldn't utter a word for the pain and pleasure he was rendering to me. One minute he was sweet with the loving, and the next he was straight savage as he was talking nice-nasty to me.

"I brought you out here for a reason, you know," he voiced as he placed my legs on his shoulders, all the while digging in my pussy.

The once pleasurable thrusts of his dick turned into not so pleasant. Not enjoying his movements, I began to scoot away from him.

"Stop motherfucking running, Jonzella," he groaned as it felt like his dick was growing bigger inside of me.

"You arc hurting me, Totta," I winced.

"You better take this dick, guh."

Let's just say that the experience was making me afraid of him as I tried to understand where his aggression came from. Tears seeped down my face as I glared into the emotionless man's eyes. I didn't know who the person was that was pounding in my pussy. Trying to go to my happy place, I couldn't—Totta wouldn't let me.

"Open your fucking eyes and look at me," he growled as he slowed his movements.

I did what he commanded.

"Watch this dick go in and out of you. No matter how I serve this dick to you, you better watch it and don't move a muscle. Do you understand?" he voiced nastily.

On the brink of crying, I nodded my head. I didn't know how long I lay on the back of his car with my legs spread as I watched Totta drill my pussy until it was sore. There was no passion in what he was doing; it was pure torture. I was glad when I felt his dick throbbing.

Pounding the fuck out of me, Totta grinned as he pressed his body further into mine all the while spreading my legs to the max. Every part of my body hurt from this man, and I had to put an end to it.

"Get the fuck off me!" I screamed as the tears slid down my cheeks.

Ignoring me, Totta continued doing his deed.

"I said, get the fuck--." My comment was cut short as he slow stroked my severely hurting twat, followed by speaking.

"I will get up when I bust this nut, Jonzella," he growled inches away from my face.

"Fuck that, get up!"

That motherfucker didn't get up until my pussy was leaking with his sperm. I was mad, hurt, and confused. The pain I felt in my pussy was not to be compared with the pain I felt in my heart. Totta's actions were never like this with me. He has never treated me as if I was just a piece of ass to him.

As he hopped from the trunk, he chuckled, followed by saying, "You are the real MVP, Jonzella. No wonder I fucked with you harder than any female that I ever fucked with."

His comment left me limp on the trunk. All I could do was stare at him with a hurt facial expression. Questions entered my brain, which I couldn't bring myself to ask him.

Handing me my clothing, Totta said, "You might want to get used to me getting on you from time to time like that."

"Why?" I heard my small voice ask.

"Because at times I need to fuck like that."

"Totta, I'm pregnant. I can't handle that type of sex," I said as I looked at him.

"Your pussy wasn't saying that," he laughed.

He was being an asshole, and I wanted to be far away from him. Thus, I began to put on my clothes. In a flash, Totta snatched me off the trunk of the car, ordered for me to touch my toes, and rammed his dick inside of me. I never felt so violated in my life. I cried the entire time he was fucking me.

"Why are you doing me like this?" I inquired as I tried to run from the dick.

"Because you need to know your damn place when you are fucking with me," he growled while slamming his dick in me while smacking my ass repeatedly.

I felt a horrible cramp in the bottom of my stomach, causing me to drop to the ground.

"Get the fuck up and take what I am giving you, Jonzella!" he barked as he pulled me by my hair.

"Nooo. Get the fuck away from me!" I yelled as I tried to fight him off.

I wasn't successful as he snatched me off the ground, carrying me to his car as I kicked and screamed for him to leave me alone. The passenger door opened, followed by Totta placing me in the front seat as he spread my legs and placed his dick into my aching hole.

"Totta, noooo!" I yelped as he placed his hands around my neck.

"You must have thought I was playing with you when I said that I would fuck you up. You must thought I was playing when I said that I love you, and I wanted you in my life. Huh?" he questioned loudly as he pounded inside of me.

"No, I didn't think you were playing," I cried as my stomach continued to hurt.

"Then why in the fuck are you texting and calling another nigga?" he voiced loudly as it felt like he was digging a hole in me.

Not expecting for him to say that, I replied, "What are you talking about?"

He didn't respond for what it seemed like forever as he savagely beat up my pussy. Thus, I asked him the question again.

"I had to use your phone last night since I dropped mine in the toilet. As I was talking to Dank, you had a lot of incoming messages. Once I got off the phone with him, I had to see who was texting you like that. To my surprise, it was one of your fucking exes you were fucking with prior to me."

"I ... can explain," I voiced as the tears flooded my face.

"Nawl, Jonzella, no need to explain sweetheart," he voiced as he pulled out of me.

"Totta, I love you. I was just lonely and needed someone to talk to."

"How in the fuck were you lonely with a sister at home, and me as your man? I was there whenever you wanted to talk ... even if I was mad at you. So, how lonely could you really have been? Or was your pussy hot for another dick since I wasn't in town much to knock that motherfucka down?

"It wasn't nothing like that, Totta," I cried.

"A'ight," he voiced as he ambled away from me.

Hopping out of the car as if I didn't have a sore pussy, I begged for Totta to listen to me. He didn't. Instead, he quickly pulled his cell phone out of his pants pocket and dialed a number.

"Totta!" I yelled as he slipped his clothes on.

"What's up?" he spoke into his phone.

Immediately, I knew he was on the phone with a bitch. I went insane as my naked tail rolled up on him, slamming my fist into his chest.

"You think you will be on the phone with a bitch while I'm in your presence. You got me fucked up, guy!"

That motherfucker continued talking as if I wasn't in his face, hitting him. Once his pants were secured, he told the broad, "Hold on a minute."

Placing his cold eyes on me, he said, "Get dressed so I can drop you off at home."

"We need to talk."

"Nawl, we good. You just showed me that bitches ain't shit."

"Coming from the nigga that had hoes at me," I spat nastily.

Ignoring me, Totta strolled towards the driver's door. I felt like shit as I knew I had no business communicating with an ex from school. I knew when I gave him my number two weeks ago that I was setting myself up for failure with my relationship with Totta.

"Oh, yeah, this relationship of ours is over with, Jonzella. I'm done with you, but not our child," he voiced after he told whomever on the phone that he would see them shortly.

"Totta, don't do this to me," I cried as I ran to the passenger door with my clothes in my hand as sperm was flowing towards my feet.

Ignoring me, he turned on the radio and rapidly backed away. All I could do was cry as I placed my clothes on my body. Not one time did Totta want to hear what I had to say. I sure as hell wasn't hearing that he was done with me. Whatever I had to do to get him back, I was going to do. I made a stupid mistake, and I really hated that I was losing the one man that was made for me.

The ride back to the city limits of Montgomery went in a blur as Totta drove his car like a bat out of hell. He didn't look my way as I kept my eyes on him. There was nothing that I could do to make him talk to me.

As he turned onto my street, Totta said, "I hope he was worth you losing me."

"Totta, listen to me. He meant nothing to me. He was just someone to converse with. It never got sexual, and I never told him that I wanted to be with him. It was strictly general conversation. Please, don't let me conversing with another man take what we have away."

"Like I told you in Hope Hull, I'm done with you but not our child," he voiced while looking sternly at me.

"I don't want us to be just co-parents," I whined as I rubbed his hand.

"Welp, you don' fucked it up. Make sure you tell the truth when folks ask why we ain't together no more."

"I made a fucking mistake. I know what I want and that's you! I will never converse with another male on my phone unless it's about school work, about our child ... basically important shit. I promise you I will never disrespect our relationship or you again."

I begged that man for over two hours to not let my stupid mistake cause us to not be together. I informed him that I was willing to do anything to make things right between us. Eventually, he gave in to what I had to say.

As we maneuvered into the house, Totta's phone began to ring.

"You better tell that bitch you are taken," I voiced loudly.

"She will know when I don't show up at her crib that I am taken."

From that moment until the wee hours of the morning, Totta made up for hurting me as I made up for bringing unnecessary drama and feelings his way. The lovemaking was sweet and passionate, just the way I liked.

"I love you and only you, Joshua Nixon," I cooed as I met his slow thrusts.

"And I love you, Jonzella Brown. Don't make me do what I did to you again. Next, time you might not be so lucky."

CHAPTER 22
Casey

Sunday, April 30ᵗʰ

This had been one interesting month. I had so much shit to do until it I was past due for a vacation. Everything had to go right with my dealings with X before I could focus heavily on transitioning to the man I was destined to be. There were plenty of nights I went to bed with a headache.

I thought those knuckleheaded niggas would've learned from the shit that happened to Danzo and two of the guys that he dealt with; I was dead wrong. After Totta and I tried to talk some sense into those niggas, we realized that they needed some shit to happen to them for them to understand what they were dealing with. The life lessons that we were telling them went in one ear and out the other. I could barely sleep for the thought of the blood that was about to be shed. Jonsey couldn't understand what I was going through mentally because I didn't fully tell her about the blood and mourning that was due to come.

The preacher cut my thoughts short when he announced that it was time for the altar call. Immediately, I knew I had to be up there giving out extensive prayer. As I stood, so did Jonsey. Connecting her hand with mine, we waltzed toward the altar. There were so many people leaving the pews for extra prayer, causing my heart to warm. The closer we came to our destination, the more I thought about the young niggas and their families, the safety and well-being of my family, and my sanity. Since it was heavy on my mind, I knew that I had to send a special prayer up. True, I was a dope boy through and through, but one thing I really hated was young niggas losing their lives over stupid shit when it all could've been avoided. All they had to do was listen to what Totta and I had to say. I couldn't understand why they couldn't live by the G-Code.

As the preacher talked, we came to a complete stop at the first pew. Bowing my head, I tuned him out and prayed for everyone. Moments passed before I lifted my head. Jonsey grabbed my hand and kissed the back of it as we strolled toward our seat.

As soon as I took a seat, Totta passed me his cellphone. With one of his eyebrows raised, I knew that it was urgent. On the screen was a text message thread from J-Money stating that we were requested at a meeting X was having at his house at two-thirty p.m.

Clearing my throat, I replied to the text message: *Will we be done by three-thirty?*

His response was: *Hell yes. It's Sunday. Chief likes to chill on the Lord's day lol.*

After handing Totta back his phone, my mind pondered what the Queenpin wanted from us. I prayed that she didn't want us to do another bid. We told her that we weren't going to be in the streets anymore.

Once the church services ended, Totta and Jonzella split off from us—going to Totta's home; whereas, Jonsey and I headed to my home. Their living situation changed the moment the ladies decided it was best that they moved in with us. Totta or I didn't object to what they had to say; instead, we helped them pack their stuff and moved it into our homes.

Breaking the lease wasn't an issue since Totta and I paid what was asked. I thought it was going to be a hard transition for the ladies not living with each other anymore; they did well. It wasn't like they didn't see each other daily. If Jonzella and Totta weren't cooking at their home, Jonsey and I were cooking. Sometimes we would dine out, eat at my grandmother's or Totta's mother's crib.

Totta and my family were glad that we were turning over a new leaf and stepping into parenthood. My grandmother, mother, and Ms. Shirl let it be known to Jonzella and Jonsey that their babies were going to be spoiled beyond belief. There was no need in Totta and me trying to talk those women out of spoiling their first grandkids.

"Did you enjoy church today?" Jonsey inquired as we stepped into our newly decorated home.

"Yes," I replied as I locked the door and set the alarm.

"Your mind has been heavy lately baby. Do you want to talk about it?" she asked as she kicked off her black and gray flats.

"Later tonight I will. Totta and I have a meeting at two-thirty," I told her as I strolled towards her.

Sighing heavily, Jonsey glared at me before speaking. "I thought you said that you were done having meetings and being in the streets."

"I am. We gotta see what has to be said. I promise you, baby, I am done with that street runner life. I'm a family man, now," I informed her as I wrapped my arms around her growing waist.

"You know we have engagements tonight at the home. Will y'all be back in time for us to take care of our business at the elderly home?"

"Yes. The meeting will only be an hour. You and Jonzella can meet Totta and me at the retirement home."

"Do you think you will get the engineering job you applied for in Hope Hull?" she inquired as she looked into my eyes.

With a huge smile on my face, I replied, "I hope so. The interview on Friday went great. I passed the assessment test Friday with flying colors. Now, all I have to do is wait for them to schedule me a second interview."

"Stay positive, and you will get the job, babe. Do you think you can handle a nine to five versus to making your own schedule?"

"It will take some time to get used to, but I'm willing to do what I have to. It will be a major adjustment, but nothing that I can't handle," I informed her as I placed a kiss on her forehead, all the rubbing on her booty.

As I was on the verge of being mannish with Jonsey, my cell phone rang. Quickly looking at my cell, I saw Totta's name displaying across the screen. Clearing my throat, I answered the phone.

"Aye, do you think the ladies need to meet us at the home?" Totta asked.

"I was just telling Jonsey that they should meet us there."

Not responding to me, Totta yelled to Jonzella what I had discussed with Jonsey. After I heard Jonzella say okay, my partner returned his attention to me.

"Are you ready to roll out and see what's up?"

"Yeah."

"A'ight. Your turn to pull up on me," he stated.

"A'ight. I'm on my way," I chuckled.

"Bet," he replied before we ended the call.

Placing my eyes on my pregnant lady, I said, "I promise you as soon as the meeting is over we are heading to the retirement home. Then, I am yours and not in the streets."

"You better be, or it will be some smoke in the city," she voiced as she kissed my lips gently.

My man was bricking up, and I knew I had no time to be fondling her oh so sweet body; thus, I groaned before I pulled away from her. Jonsey chuckled as I ran towards our room. Within fifteen minutes, my church attire was on the bed as I had on casual clothing. Before I dashed downstairs, I checked my appearance in the mirror. Satisfied with my look, I told Jonsey that I would see her as soon as the meeting was over with.

The ride to Totta's house didn't take long as it seemed like all the traffic lights were on green. Honking the horn, his black ass skipped out the door buttoning up his pants.

Shaking my head, I rolled down my window and asked, "Damn, you can't go five minutes without getting some pussy, nigga? You act like you ain't never had none before."

Laughing, he yelled, "Shut up, nigga."

Hopping in my front seat, Totta asked, "What do you think this meeting is about?"

"I don't know, but I hope she ain't coming to us about being on her team or no shit like that. You know she will blackmail us to do whatever she needs done, and I am not prepared or equipped to go up against her," I told him as I backed away from the parking spot.

"I'm hoping she just on some good shit, and then we can be on our way. I'm already in the doghouse with Jonzella as she is in the doghouse with me. The last thing I need is for us to be on some more shit," he stated as I hopped in traffic, aiming for J-Money's crib.

"What in the hell popped off between the two of y'all anyway?"

Totta began telling me what happened between him and Jonzella some days ago. I knew that their relationship was thrown off, but I didn't know why. They barely talked to each other, yet they were doing a lot of fucking. Honestly, I didn't see how they were mad at each other if all they did was screw and tell each other that they loved one another.

Once Totta finished telling me what took place between him and Jonzella, I shook my head and said, "Wow."

I didn't understand one bit why she had to be conversing with an ex when she proclaimed that Totta was all that she needed. I wasn't going to put my two cents where it didn't belong; the same thing that I preached to Jonsey in the beginning of our relationship was the same statement I was going to live by.

"Do you think I was wrong for how I reacted to her?" Totta inquired as we were close to J-Money's crib.

"I'm not going to answer that. If you feel like you had to do what you did...then so be it," I told him as I pulled onto the curb in front of J-Money's home.

I was glad that he left the conversation alone. I was not going to indulge in his lings with Jonzella for what she did.

"Let's get this over with. We have engagements that we must take care of, then I'mma be ready to turn in it for the night," Totta voiced as he hopped out of the passenger seat.

Agreeing with him, I observed J-Money's home as it had two black Tahoes and The Beast parked in the driveway. The aroma coming from the house was on wham; someone was inside cooking their asses off, which made my stomach growl. I was eager to get inside as I knocked on the screen door.

In a matter of seconds, a stern-faced Ruger opened the door with a weak ass hello.

Chuckling, I replied, "What up, mane."

Of course, he was closed lipped. Strolling through the threshold of the door, Totta and I spoke to The Savage Clique and the woman of the house. She was a cute, petite woman who didn't take any shit from the goofy as dude I considered to be a chill as nigga.

"What's up, fellas?" X stated as she took a sip from her bottle water.

As we dapped the rest of the fellas up, Totta answered her question. "We cooling before it's time for us to head down to the retirement home to cook for the elderly peeps."

"That's what's up," she replied happily as she stood.

"Who stinkin' up the grill like that?" I asked, looking around.

"Baked," Silky Snake raspy's voice stated.

"Okay den," Totta voiced.

"I won't keep y'all long. I just want to touch base with y'all for a brief second," X announced as she motioned for us to follow her.

As soon as we strolled out of the back door, my stomach damn near touched the ground. I was hungry as hell! I knew I was going to get me a plate; I wasn't going to have it no other way.

"Fellas, I called y'all out here because I wanted to personally hand y'all funds, congratulate y'all once again on being fathers, and to tell y'all that I appreciate everything that you have done for me. If y'all ever get in a pickle, please don't hesitate to call me," she stated sincerely as she looked Totta and I in the face.

"No problem, and thank you for helping us out," we stated in unison.

"With that being said, there you go," X voiced as DB handed Totta and me two nice-sized duffle bags.

Instantly, I wondered how much money was in the bags. Apparently, I had a weird facial expression because The Savage Clique minus Ruger laughed.

"One bag is filled with your earnings, and the other is filled with neutral gender baby items," she voiced proudly with a pleasant smile on her face.

A nigga was filled with emotions as I ambled towards the hard ass woman who really had a soft side.

Wrapping my arms around her, I told her thank you, followed by whispering in her ear, "You can leave and be happy, also. You can have a family. Get out while you still can. Much love and blessings, X."

***

It was ten o'clock when Jonsey and I snuggled in the bed. We had an amazing time at the retirement home. Totta and I helped the elderly men with their grooming and attire. The ladies held a makeover in the elderly women's wing, which was the main damn reason why it took a while for them to come down and help Totta and me with dinner preparations.

I couldn't lie and say I didn't like how the elderly women looked when the stepped into the dining hall; even though, they were old women you could tell that they were gorgeous in their younger days.

A couple of disturbances popped off when, Mrs. Wilson took too long to finish her prayer, followed by her wanting to be the center of attention. One thing about Mrs. Wilson was that she didn't like to share me with any of the women in the retirement home. She would be quick to tell them to get their own guy who comes and visits them.

After dinner, we played different board and card games. Close to the ending of dinner, Mrs. Wilson slipped off with Jonsey. Thirty minutes later, Jonsey appeared with tears running down her face as she held a joyful smile on her face.

"Aye, Jonsey, you never did tell me what happened after you left from with Mrs. Wilson," I stated as I rubbed the small of her back.

"She gave me her mother's pearl necklace and bracelet, followed by telling me that I better take care of you because you deserve to be with someone that loves you unconditionally. She gave me her blessing to be with you when she's not present."

Bursting out in laughter, I shook my head. "That woman is something else."

"She sure is, yet, she's sweet as she can be. How did you meet her?"

"She was in the hot ass heat some years ago, and I couldn't let her continue to walk knowing she was old. So, I pulled over and asked her where she was going. Along the way, we chatted. She told me about her nothing ass son…who lives in the city and barely visits her or take her where she has to go. Something in my spirit told me to step up and be what her son wasn't to her, and I have kept my end of the deal."

Rolling on top of me, Jonsey rained kiss over my face while she repeatedly told me that she loved me.

"I love you, too, woman," I voiced as I squeezed her booty.

"I don't want your sweet ways to change for nothing. Do you hear me?"

"Never," I voiced before parting her mouth with my tongue.

Our kissing led us into a passionate filled night.

When we were done, I asked Jonsey, "How can you love me so much after all that we have been through?"

"Cuz' I got caught up in a d-boy's illest love…that's why," she replied before sucking on my bottom lip.

"Is that so?" I inquired while placing my head on her shoulders.

"Yep."

"Have you talked to your father or brother?"

"I talked to Kyvin yesterday, and as far as my father goes…I meant what I said. I'm done with him."

"And he's okay with it?" I asked curiously.

"According to Jonzella, he's okay with it. She gives him updates about me. Why are you asking me these questions?"

"Because you haven't said one thing about them or your mom. By the way, how's she doing?"

Shrugging her shoulders, she replied, "Don't know and I don't care."

Seeing that she was getting agitated, I left that conversation alone. She was hell bent on not communicating with her parents. I did pray in time that she at least forgave them.

Pulling her close to me, I said, "You do know you are my world, right?"

"As you are mine."

ABOUT THE NOVELIST

TN Jones was born in Montgomery, Alabama, but raised in Prattville, Alabama. She currently resides in Montgomery, Alabama with her daughter. Growing up, TN Jones always had a passion for reading and writing, which led her to writing short stories.

In 2015, TN Jones began working on her first book, *Disloyal: Revenge of a Broken Heart*, which was previously titled, *Passionate Betrayals*.

TN Jones does not have a set genre she writes in. She will write in the following genres: Women's fiction, Mystery/Suspense, Urban fiction, Dark Erotica/Erotica, and Urban/Interracial Paranormal.

Published by TN Jones: *Disloyal: Revenge of a Broken Heart, Disloyal 2-3: A Woman's Revenge, A Sucka in Love for a Thug, If You'll Give Me Your Heart 1-2, By Any Means: Going Against the*

Grain 1-2, Choosing To Love a Lady Thug 1-3, and *The Sins of Love: Finessing the Enemies 1-2.*

Upcoming novels by TN Jones*: The Sins of Love 3: Finessing the Enemies, Choosing To Love a Lady Thug 4, Is This Your Man, Sis: Side Piece Chronicles,* and *I Now Pronounce You, Mr. and Mrs. Thug.*

Thank you for reading the final installment of *Caught Up In a D-Boy's Illest Love.* Please leave an honest review under the book title on Amazon's page.

For future book details, please visit any of the following links below:

Amazon Author page: https://www.amazon.com/tnjones666

Facebook: https://www.facebook.com/novelisttnjones/

Goodreads:
https://www.goodreads.com/author/show/14918893.TN_Jones:

Google+:
https://www.plus.google.com/u/1/communities/115057649956960897339

Instagram: https://www.instagram.com/tnjones666

Twitter: https://twitter.com/TNHarris6.

You are welcome to email her: tnjones666@gmail.com; as well as chat with her daily in her Facebook group, **It's Just Me...TN Jones**.

CPSIA information can be obtained
at www.ICGtesting.com
Printed in the USA
LVHW091739191219
641092LV00002B/244/P